Where in the world is Stu Frysley?

"Any luck?" Mildred asked.

"Nope. No Stu," Agatha said. "We couldn't find him anywhere."

Orville didn't see what that had to do with Mildred's question, but the head counselor nodded.

"You guys, if Stu really was really snatched by Ax Jack," Adam Fratto said, "isn't he gonna get . . . you know . . ." Adam mimed swooshing an ax through the air.

"Stu's being a jerk," Counselor Clark said. "Ax Jack doesn't have him."

"If that's true, Orville and I can definitely find the little rat boy," Agatha said. "We have a one hundred percent success rate."

"Let them do it," Adam suggested. "Let them find Stu. Otherwise, the teachers will send us all home. The camping trip will be ruined."

Clark and Mildred stared at each other.

"Okay," Mildred finally said. "But you only have until the end of the day today to find him."

"No problem," Agatha said. "We'll find Stu by lunchtime. Guaranteed!"

"What if Stu's not playing a trick?" Orville asked. "What if you're wrong and he really is in trouble?"

Agatha's eyes widened. "That's not possible . . . is it?"

The **Wright &
Wong** Mysteries

Wright & Wong

The Case of the Trail Mix-Up

Laura J. Burns & Melinda Metz

SLEUTH
RAZORBILL

Wright & Wong 3: The Case of the Trail Mix-Up

RAZORBILL

Published by the Penguin Group
Penguin Young Readers Group
345 Hudson Street, New York, New York 10014, U.S.A.
Penguin Group (USA) Inc., 375 Hudson Street, New York, New York 10014, U.S.A.
Penguin Group (Canada), 90 Eglinton Avenue, Suite 700, Toronto, Ontario, Canada M4P 2Y3
(a division of Pearson Penguin Canada Inc.)
Penguin Books Ltd, 80 Strand, London WC2R 0RL, England
Penguin Ireland, 25 St Stephen's Green, Dublin 2, Ireland (a division of Penguin Books Ltd)
Penguin Group (Australia), 250 Camberwell Road, Camberwell, Victoria 3124, Australia
(a division of Pearson Australia Group Pty Ltd)
Penguin Books India Pvt Ltd, 11 Community Centre, Panchsheel Park,
New Delhi - 110 017, India
Penguin Group (NZ), Cnr Airborne and Rosedale Roads, Albany, Auckland 1310,
New Zealand (a division of Pearson New Zealand Ltd)
Penguin Books (South Africa) (Pty) Ltd, 24 Sturdee Avenue, Rosebank,
Johannesburg 2196, South Africa

Penguin Books Ltd, Registered Offices: 80 Strand, London WC2R 0RL, England

10 9 8 7 6 5 4 3 2 1

Interior design by Christopher Grassi

Library of Congress Cataloging-in-Publication Data is available

Printed in the United States of America

Chapter 1

"You brought your creamed corn. You have your Oreos. That means your dinners at camp will be a quarter regular and only two-thirds new," Agatha Wong told her best friend, Orville Wright.

"One-quarter and two-thirds equals eleven-twelfths. You have one-twelfth unaccounted for," Orville replied. "And there is no mathematical method for calculating the loss of my kitchen table and my usual dinner timeline in your equation." Orville turned to gaze out the window of the bus.

Agatha nodded and tried not to smile. So she wasn't a math head. But she had absorbed enough numbers to know how to screw up fractions on purpose. And she figured screwing up fractions would distract Orville—at least a tiny bit. Orville needed distraction. Big time. Because right now he—and the rest of the seventh-grade class of John Q. Adams Middle School—were on a big Trixie the Sea Monster purple bus. Since Trixie was a girl, Agatha thought she should be called a Sea Monster*ess*. She tried it often. But the phrase never caught on. Nana Wong said it was because people feared change.

In any case, the girlness or boyness of Trixie wasn't the problem. The problem was that the bus was taking Orville to South Haven County Park for a camping trip. South Haven was only a fifteen-minute drive from Bottomless Lake. But those few minutes seriously messed with Orville's routine. And messing with Orville's routine *seriously* messed with Orville's head. Orville had Asperger's syndrome, which meant that, among other things, he liked his routine to stick to the routine. Orville sat still in his bus seat, staring straight ahead with a kind of blank expression on his face. To most people, he looked calm. That was one of the effects of Asperger's syndrome—Orville couldn't show emotions on the outside. But inside, Agatha could tell he was freaking out.

"I can't believe we've never been camping before," Agatha continued, keeping up the distraction. "We're truly underprivileged. I mean it. I may take my parents to court for mistreating me. That is, I would if they were home enough to mistreat me."

Orville turned to look at Agatha. "Your mom and dad will return from Bangladesh in one hundred and two hours and twenty-four minutes."

Agatha nodded. Orville knew she hated the fact that her folks traveled so much on business. That was his way of trying to comfort her. "I blame Nana Wong, then," Agatha insisted. "She's my, whatchamacallit? My primary caretaker. And she should have taken me camping by now. Don't you think?"

Agatha waited for an answer. Orville understood that if a person paused long enough in a conversation, it normally meant that they expected a reply. Orville wasn't a big talker. If he hadn't learned rules like that, he'd probably never have talked at all. Instead, he preferred to think. And calculate. And think some more. He didn't see the point in pointless conversation, and Agatha was happy to do most of the talking anyway. People often asked her if she enjoyed the sound of her own voice. And the answer was Yes, very much, thank you. But with Orville nearing his freakage point, Agatha didn't want him off in his head thinking who-knew-what. She wanted him front and center.

"I don't think Nana Wong had a legal obligation to—" Orville began.

"I know that," Agatha interrupted. "The court thing? That was just me being me. You know I exaggerate. I just meant that South Haven is supposed to be perfect for weekend getaways. Don't you think it will be fun to go camping there?"

"South Haven has been called the jewel of the extensive county park system. It has a two-mile-wide lake and more than fifty miles of rivers and streams. Seventy-one percent of the park falls within the White Mountain range." Orville quoted from memory the

brochure their teacher had sent home with their permission slips.

"I'll take that as a big 'heck, yeah,'" Agatha said. "It's
a great place to camp."

"Your friend looks a little twitchy," Agatha heard a
voice say. It was a familiar voice. A hideously familiar
voice. A second later the face and body attached to the
voice lurched into the aisle between Agatha and
Orville's seats.

"He's not going to puke, is he?" Stu Frysley asked,
ignoring Orville completely. Agatha had to admit maybe
this was a happy thing. Stu usually let something awful,
like the word *retard*, slip out of his mouth when he spoke
to Orville for more than a few seconds. It had been that
way since time began, all the way back to the second
grade. And it continued to this day, even though Agatha
and Orville had recently saved Stu's pathetic pink behind.

Stu Frysley had done one good thing in his life, even
though he hadn't meant to do it. He was the reason
Agatha had ended up with the bestest best friend ever.
Because back when they were little, Stu had been such a
weenie head to Orville that Agatha (who used to like to
think of herself as a superhero called the Avengenator)
had felt compelled to go to the rescue. And the rest was
sweet history.

"Oh my gosh! Did Stu say Orville's going to puke?"
Erin Shoffer asked.

Agatha calmly shook her head. "The only reason anybody on this bus is going to go vomitous is Stuey's breath." She sniffed dramatically. "What have you been eating?"

"She's right!" somebody from the very back of the bus called. "I can smell you from here!"

"It's just trail mix." Stu pulled a plastic bag out of his jacket pocket and gave it a shake. "Marshmallows, rainbow sprinkles, pearl onions, and Cheez Doodles. I made it myself."

Moans and groans erupted from everybody within earshot. Clark Frysley, Stu's cousin, got up from his seat at the front of the bus and wobbled down the aisle to Stu. Clark was one of the high school counselors for the camping trip. "Um, so, is there a problem down here?" he asked.

"Is there a problem down here?" Stu mocked in a falsetto voice.

Agatha sighed. You could take the boy out of the kindergarten, but you couldn't take the kindergarten out of the boy. Stu would probably be just as immature when he was eighty as he was right now.

Clark rolled his eyes. "You heard me, Stu," he said. "What's the ruckus?"

"What's the ruckus?" Stu repeated.

Clark glanced around the bus. Everyone was watching now.

"That's all you can come up with? 'Ruckus'?" Stu went on, enjoying the attention. "That's your dad's word! You're just doing an imitation of your dad!"

Clark swallowed so hard, Agatha could see his Adam's apple go up and down.

"Can you believe I have to stay with this loser for the next two weeks?" Stu asked everyone within earshot. "You'd think my parents could at least find me a cooler babysitter if they had to go on vacation."

Agatha waited for Clark's response. It was so obvious that he should point out that only babies needed babysitters. But Clark just blushed. Wow. That was no way to deal with the horror that was Stu Frysley.

"Is there a problem or not?" Clark asked, his voice squeaking.

"You're my problem!" Stu cried.

Agatha wondered how Orville was doing on the other side of the cousin-versus-cousin confrontation. She couldn't even see him across the aisle. Clark and Stu were blocking her view.

"Listen, Stu—"

"Does anybody want to hear a story?" Stu interrupted. "It's about our counselor, Clark. Clark's nickname is—"

"Don't—" Clark protested.

Stu ignored him. "It's Linguini. Because when he was little, he—"

Clark slapped his hand over Stu's mouth. The bus bounced, and they both hit the floor with a *thwack*, Stu on top of Clark. Stu grabbed one of Clark's hands and used it to whap Clark in the face. "Why are you hitting yourself? Why are you hitting yourself?" Stu cackled. Clark rolled over so that he had Stu pinned beneath him. Everybody for ten seats around jumped up to get a better view of the fight. Agatha expected Clark to pummel Stu since he was so much bigger and older. But now that he was on top, Clark didn't seem to know what to do. Agatha glanced over at Orville. He looked fine, although he had backed up in his seat to avoid being hit by the flailing limbs of Stu and Clark.

The head counselor, Mildred Bennett, rushed over wearing an eagle-who's-spotted-a-mouse expression on her face. She was only a senior in high school, but with that expression she could easily have passed for a teacher.

"Get up!" Mildred ordered, grabbing Clark by the back of his shirt. She glanced over her shoulder. "Mr. Andersen is sleeping and Ms. Winogrand is reading some gross horror book. They haven't noticed that you one, failed to get this camper back into his seat, and two, pinned him bodily to the ground."

"Sorry," Clark muttered. He scrambled to his feet and helped Stu up.

"Clark, I know you want to be head counselor next

year," Mildred said. "Well, memo: this is not the way I got the job. And it's not why I'm going to Yellowstone with the other head counselors from Arizona next month." Mildred shook her head. Her expression had gone mama-dog-with-annoying-pup. "Get it together. I don't care if he *is* your cousin—it's just not the appropriate time for this roughhousing."

"Return to your seat, camper," Clark told Stu. He smoothed down his blond hair. But there was nothing he could do about the bright red splotches on his cheeks. Well, nothing that wouldn't have involved a lot of makeup.

"Fine," Stu said. He took his time walking back to his spot on the bus. And Agatha heard him mutter, "Linguini," under his breath before he sat down.

Agatha leaned across the aisle to whisper to Orville. "Who knew they were going to provide entertainment on the big purple bus? This camping trip is awesome already."

Ten minutes later, the bus had parked and everyone was busy setting up tents. Agatha hurried to get her share of the work done. She wanted to check on Orville. But first she needed to make sure her sleeping bag ended up in a tent *not* occupied by Ms. Winogrand. Ms. Wino sent the arrow in the Agatha Wong like-o-meter as far over into the red zone as it could go. There was no way Agatha was sleeping anywhere near her least-favorite person. Well, Stu might be her least-favorite person. But Ms. Wino was definitely her least-favorite teacher.

She watched until she saw Ms. Winogrand haul her stuff into the tent closest to the bathrooms, which Mildred had been calling "latrines." As soon as Ms. Wino and her purple hair were out of sight, Agatha tossed her bag into the tent farthest away from hers and then went to find Orville by the campfire.

Orville stared at her. He wasn't usually down with the staring. He didn't like eye contact. "What?" Agatha asked.

"I am trying to think of something to compliment you on," Orville explained.

"And you're having trouble?"

"Yes."

Orville!

"That's not very—" Then Agatha got it. "This is an assignment from your social skills class, isn't it?"

"Yes. Miss Eloise says people enjoy being complimented. What would you like to be complimented on?"

"There are so many things you can choose from. I'm ridiculously complimentworthy." Orville continued to look at her.

"How about my hair?" Agatha suggested. "I spend loads of time making my hair look tousled and pretty. I always appreciate a good hair compliment."

"Your hair looks tousled and pretty," Orville said.

"Really?" Agatha smiled. "You're not just saying that? Thank you so much!"

"I *am* just saying that," Orville clarified. "I told you it was an assignment less than thirty seconds ago."

Agatha sighed, deflated. Why did her best friend take everything so literally?

Orville turned his attention to the barbecue pits. The counselors and teachers were grilling hot dogs. "There's no chicken," he worried. "I always have chicken for dinner."

"True, but you've still got your creamed corn and your Oreos," Agatha reminded him. "So you've got two-thirds of your usual dinner. Right?"

Orville sighed. "Right."

"Come on. Let's get in the chow line. I've got a rumbly in my tumbly." Agatha led the way over to the clump of kids waiting for hot dogs. From the getting of the food to the eating of the food, she kept up a raging river of conversation—about the fact that her cousin Serena had to retake the SATs, why liquid soap grossed Agatha out, why Agatha's uncle Boonie grossed her out, why water tasted better when you drank it in the middle of the night, why pets should not have human names. Agatha hoped it would help Orville forget that he wasn't having his usual din-din. Orville just listened and didn't worry. So far, her plan was working.

She kept up the chatter through the cleaning up after the eating of the food. Then Clark Frysley took over for her.

"Okay, campers. Get those marshmallows onto your sticks and move in closer to the fire," Clark called. "It's time for a story."

"A story? What are we, six?" Stu complained.

"A story about Ax Jack, the most cold-blooded killer who ever walked this earth," Clark continued.

"Ax Jack! My dad told me about him!" Brad Purcell called from the other side of the fire.

"I bet he didn't tell you everything. The whole story . . ." Clark shook his head. "You know what? Maybe you're right. It's probably not a story I should tell to middle school kids. It's probably too intense."

"If you can handle it, we can handle it," Stu called out. "You squealed like a little girl when we rented *Freaky Friday*." He pointed at his cousin. "He thought it was scary when Lindsay Lohan switched bodies with her mom. That's how much of a chicken Clark is."

Agatha had to admit that did sound pretty *cluck-cluck*.

"I didn't squeal," Clark protested. He was growing those red spots on his cheeks again.

"Yes, you—" Stu began.

"Why did you rent *Freaky Friday*?" Brad asked Stu. "Isn't that a girl movie?"

"Tell the story, Clark," Stu ordered, changing the subject.

Agatha stuck a marshmallow on a stick and held it close to the flames. She liked her mallows charred on the outside and all soft white gooeyness on the inside. Orville liked his an even golden brown all around the outside, and only medium-level gooey on the inside.

"Ax Jack's parents—Crazy Jenny and Chainsaw Chandler—were both mental patients at an insane asylum in Texas. And not just any insane asylum. The Thornwell Asylum. Thornwell is out in the middle of the desert. The only living beings around are rattlers and coyotes. And even these creatures flee when they hear the wild screams and shrieking laughter coming from inside Thornwell's walls."

Clark pulled in a deep breath and continued. "At Thornwell, the straitjackets have reinforced stitching. The rooms have double rows of bars. The guards carry cattle prods. There is more security than there is in Sing Sing—the prison that houses the most vicious criminals in the country. That's because the inmates at Thornwell are more dangerous than any serial killer ever convicted."

Agatha heard a little gasp. Then she realized the little gasp had come from her.

"When Crazy Jenny became pregnant with Ax Jack,

she and Chandler decided there was no way their child was going to be born on the inside," Clark continued. "They were getting out of the asylum—no matter who or what stood in their way.

"Jenny and Chandler led a rebellion. The inmates were drenched in dark red blood—and I'm not talking about their own—by the time they burst through the fence around the asylum. But they were free." Clark stared into the fire, as if he could see Ax Jack's parents in the flames. "They set themselves up in a little trailer park. They were so proud of their son, Jack. The way he started out stomping on ants, then moved on to creating traps for bigger animals. When he was in high school, he made himself an ax in wood shop class. And the day he finished, he used that ax—on his teacher."

"Bottomless Lake has a town ordinance against students making weapons of any kind in a school setting," Orville whispered. "I would say there is an eighty-five percent chance they have similar ordinances in Texas."

"It's just a story," Agatha whispered back. "Everyone knows Ax Jack doesn't exist."

"Of course, Ax Jack was arrested," Clark continued. "They were going to strap him into the electric chair for what he did. But on the way to prison, Ax Jack escaped. And he didn't even have an ax. He had to use his bare hands to take down his police escort. And his teeth. One of the policemen lost a thumb that day. Ax Jack bit it right off."

Agatha pulled her marshmallow out of the fire and popped it into her mouth. Just right. "Could that really happen?" she asked Orville. "Could a person bite off a thumb?" Having Orville as a friend was like having constant access to the Internet.

"Humans sacrificed jaw strength for big brains," Orville answered. "In humans there are fewer muscles pulling on and attached to the cranial bone. It makes our bite weaker, but it allows our skull case to be bigger. Which means bigger brains can fit in our heads."

"Ax Jack now lives in the shadows of the White Mountains. These mountains right here, rising up behind our campsite," Clark continued. "He keeps making new axes. And every time he makes one, he uses it on somebody else."

"I heard he chopped up six people on Thanksgiving Day, then went home and ate turkey!" Raina Putter exclaimed.

Clark nodded. "And he washed it down with a shake made from blueberries and the blood of his victims." Clark popped a marshmallow into his mouth, then spit it out. "Ooh, ow. Hot! I 'urned my 'ongue."

Stu shook his head. "Linguini, Linguini, Linguini.

The family hasn't put roasting marshmallows on the list of things you're allowed to do by yourself." He stabbed a marshmallow with a stick. "I'll make a nice one for you."

Clark frowned at his cousin. "Here's something else you have to know about those six murdered people— and all Ax Jack's other victims. He doesn't kill them right away." Clark waited.

"Why not?" Agatha burst out.

"There's a certain sound that old Jack likes to hear when he uses his ax. A nice, crisp crack. He's come up with a vitamin pill that gets his victims' neck bones in just the right condition to make that sound."

Clark snapped a branch and Agatha jumped. Well, not jumped, exactly. Just shifted her weight. Yeah. That was all. Just found a more comfortable position.

"Ax Jack makes his victims take these special vitamins for two days before he kills them. For two days, they must wait, knowing the ax of Jack will soon be swinging and their heads will soon be rolling and their bodies will be dumped in the ravine behind Ax Jack's place."

"Clarkie, here's a nice marshmallow for you," Stu jumped in. "Not too hot. I tested it on my wrist. That's what you do with a baby's bottle, right?"

That got some snickers and giggles. It just made Agatha want to go Avengenator on Stu. She was trying to enjoy the delicious scariness of Clark's story, and Stu was ruining it for her.

"I heard that he can chop off someone's head with one stroke of his ax," Mike Iburg volunteered.

Clark leaned closer to the fire, and the shadows leapt across his face. Reflections of the orange flames flickered in his eyes. He didn't look like Stu's kinda lame-o cousin anymore. He looked like someone who should be in the Thornwell Asylum.

"Here's something you might not have heard," he said. "Ax Jack has made friends with the wolves in the mountains. They recognize that he is the same as they are. That he is a ruthless killer."

Agatha tried to put another marshmallow on her stick. But her hand started shaking, and she jabbed her finger instead. This story was too intense to listen to while operating heavy machinery!

"We're in Ax Jack's territory right now. When we're out hiking tomorrow, if anyone hears voices, you have to let me know right away."

"Why?" Stu demanded.

"Because when you get close to Ax Jack's cabin, you can hear the moans of his victims. And none of you want to be that close to Ax Jack. If you hear those moans, run. Run . . . and pray," Clark explained. "Now it's time to hit your sleeping bags. We have an early day tomorrow."

Agatha shivered. She knew the story was full-on bogus, but she shivered anyway. Either she was scared, or it had gotten colder out as Clark told the story. She might have just shivered because it was cold. Yeah. That was it. Coldness. "Kind of a goofy story, huh, Orville?" she asked.

"I don't believe there is any combination of vitamins that would cause the neck vertebrae to make a louder cracking sound. And rattlesnakes have no ears, so they would probably not be affected by the laughter or shrieks of the inmates in the Thornwell Asylum," Orville answered.

"Good to know," Agatha said. Very good, when it was so close to beddy-bye time. "See you in the morning, Orville."

But he was already walking away. "Orville, goodbye."

He turned back toward her. "Goodbye."

Agatha gave a nod of satisfaction. She didn't really care if he said goodbye or not. But it was a social skills thing he was supposed to practice.

"Oh, hey, and if you see an old man with a gray beard and a long tan coat with green hiking boots, you better run even faster," Clark yelled from the campfire. "Because that means you're face-to-face with the killer himself."

Agatha shivered again. She hated that. *It's just because it's cold out here*, she told herself. *It's very, very cold.*

She joined the other girls in the toothbrushing/pj-putting-on/going-to-bed drill. About fifteen minutes later, she was zipped into her sleeping bag. In the dark. Thinking about Ax Jack.

It wasn't exactly what she wanted her mind to be on before she hit dreamland. Agatha pictured the most innocent thing she could. A rubber ducky. Yellow. With an orange bill. And an ax.

No! No ax.

Agatha flipped over on her back. She turned her pillow over to the cool side. Much better. She concentrated on making her breathing slow and even. In and out. In and out. Her body began to relax. In and out. In and out.

Wait. Someone else was breathing. Well, lots of people were. All the girls in her tent. But someone else was breathing really, really close. Someone was leaning over her and breathing. Agatha's body went rigid.

She didn't want to open her eyes. But she knew she had to. She willed her eyelids up.

And saw Ax Jack standing over her.

Why is Agatha screaming? Orville wondered.

"Mildred, there's a boy in our tent!" Rachel Loiacono bleated.

Was that why Agatha was screaming? Because he was a boy? But she didn't usually scream when she saw him.

And she'd known he was a boy for years.

"Orville!" Agatha exclaimed.

"Yes," Orville said.

"Hold it right there." Mildred crawled out of her sleeping bag and pointed a flashlight at him. "Now what's this about? Why are you in this tent? Because, memo: boys are not allowed in the girls' tents for any reason."

Orville blinked. No one had mentioned that rule at any time during the bus ride or the campfire. It didn't make sense to spring a rule on people out of the blue like this. "I needed to tell my friend something important," he explained.

"And it couldn't have waited until the morning?" Mildred asked.

"It could have," Orville answered.

"Then please leave," Mildred said.

"Wait!" Agatha jumped to her feet. "He means that it's possible for him to wait and tell me in the morning but not that it's a good idea. He wouldn't have come in here if it weren't a crisis situation." She turned to Orville. "So, what is it? What's the scoop?"

Orville's brain translated Agatha's question into logical language. "Someone came into our tent and took Stu."

"What?" Agatha and Mildred yelped together.

"Someone came into our tent and took Stu," Orville repeated.

"What are you talking about? Does Clark know?" Mildred demanded.

"He was sleeping. So there is almost no chance he does," Orville answered.

"You take me over there right now, mister!" Mildred spoke directly to Orville, but Agatha followed the two of them out of their tent and over to the one Orville shared with seven of the other guys and Clark. Mildred barged right in.

Orville frowned. If there was a rule that no boys could be in the girls' tents, it seemed extremely likely that the opposite rule also existed—no girls in the boys' tents. Maybe the rules didn't apply to Mildred because she was the head counselor. But in that case, Mildred would have been the only girl allowed in his tent. And Agatha had already disappeared inside.

Agatha stuck her head back out of the tent flap and snapped her fingers near Orville's face. It was their way for her to snap him out of his "zone-outs."

"I wasn't zoning out," he told her.

"Oh." Agatha grimaced. "Sorry. Get in here!"

Orville lifted the flap and stepped into the tent. Mildred was shining a flashlight at a sleeping bag. "Clark, wake up!" she ordered.

"Mom, I took out the garbage *last* night," Clark whined.

Mildred gave him a light kick. "One, I am not your mother. And two, this is about something much more important than garbage."

Clark sat up. "Mildred?"

"Have you managed to misplace one of your campers?" She turned to Orville. "This boy says someone came and took Stu. I suspect he dreamed that thanks to your ridiculous story. But I want to make sure Stu's accounted for anyway."

"It wasn't a dream," Orville said. There were key distinctions between the waking state and sleep in the areas of gross brain wave activity, muscle tone, and eye movement. Not that he could have accurately calculated his brain wave activity. Although if he tried—

Agatha was snapping again. Orville looked up at her. "What?"

She pointed to Mildred and Clark. They were staring at Stu's empty sleeping bag with their mouths hanging open. "He's gone," Clark said.

"He's really gone," Mildred said.

"I told them he was gone," Orville told Agatha. He didn't understand why their expressions indicated surprise.

She planted her hands on her hips. "Explain to them what you saw, Orville."

"I woke up. I don't remember why. I looked at my watch. Then I saw that a man was dragging Stu out of the tent."

"Why didn't you wake me up?" Clark cried.

A couple of the guys sat up. "What's going on?"

Adam Fratto asked.

"I went to get Agatha," Orville answered.

"Why?" Clark's voice was seventy-three percent higher than usual.

"Because we handle things together," Agatha answered.

"Can you describe this man?" Mildred asked.

"Go, Orville," Agatha urged. "Do your stuff."

"He was five feet, seven inches tall," Orville began. "He had a gray beard that extended four inches from the end of his chin. He—"

"Was he wearing a tan coat?" Adam shouted.

"Yes," Orville answered.

"It was Ax Jack!" Adam exclaimed.

"Ax Jack doesn't exist," Agatha told him. "Only babies believe in him."

"Oh, okay. Well, tell us this, Orville, did this guy have a bottle of vitamins?" Adam asked.

"Yes," Orville answered.

"And green hiking boots?" Adam demanded. His voice was higher than usual too. Eighty-seven percent, Orville decided.

"Yes. Very large green hiking boots. I would estimate size sixteen."

"Did he have an ax?" Agatha asked.

"Yes," Orville said.

"It has to be Ax Jack," Adam muttered. "Has to be.

The guy had an ax. Who walks around with an ax? Ax Jack, that's who." He was talking forty-four times faster than usual.

"Or it could be somebody pretending to be Ax Jack," Agatha suggested. "Somebody who's heard the stories we all have."

"That's logical," Orville agreed. "The odds of a man with a gray beard appearing in our tent with an ax, wearing a long tan coat and green hiking boots, carrying vitamins, *without* intending to look like Ax Jack are extremely low."

"Right. If you were going to come in here and snatch Stu, you could just wear a black ski mask—anything to cover your face," Agatha went on. "But our Stu-snatcher chose to do the snatching dressed as Ax Jack. That's an important clue."

"What are you, a detective?" Mildred asked.

"Actually, yes," Agatha answered. "Orville and I have solved two humongously challenging cases. And we're happy to take on the job of finding Stu. Not that we want him back. But we're detectives. It's what we do."

"They *did* find out who stole my aunt's Harley-Davidson plate," Clark said.

Adam added, "They're actually good."

"I resent the *actually*," Agatha told him. "But thank you anyway."

"What do you think?" Clark asked. "Do we let them try? Or do we go wake up the teachers and—"

"Oh. Oh, oh!" Agatha waved her hand in the air, like she was dying to answer a question in class. "My brain is on fire! I know what happened. And it has nothing to do with Ax Jack. Because as we all know, there is no Ax Jack!"

"Ax Jack was just in our tent," Adam insisted.

Agatha shook her head. "Stu the Stinky just played an enormous prank on us. And we all fell for it."

"What are you talking about?" Clark asked. He ran his fingers through his blond hair until it was standing up in thirteen different directions.

"I'm talking about Stu being Stu. He punked us. He wants us to think Ax Jack grabbed him and get all scared," Agatha explained.

"Agatha, I saw someone pull Stu out of the tent. Someone who wasn't Stu," Orville reminded her.

"Someone with an ax and vitamins and green boots," Adam jumped in. "Somebody named Ax Jack."

"So Stu got someone to help him," Agatha said. "Even Stu has a few friends. I suspect he pays them."

Mildred turned to Clark. "He's your cousin. What do you think?"

"Stu knows how much I want to be head counselor next year. If I reported him missing, it would totally mess that up for me. Which he would love." Clark scratched the back of his neck. "The whole thing does sound pretty Stu."

"We're supposed to get everybody up at six. It's a little after five now. Let's do a quick search before we decide anything. Quick and quiet," Mildred said. "Just the people in this tent and my tent who are awake. Meet back at the barbecue grills in half an hour. And I did say quiet, right?"

Clark handed out flashlights. Agatha and Orville stepped outside and pointed their lights at the ground. "We should have told the others to let us go out first," Agatha said. "They trampled over any tracks those moose-size hiking boots would have left."

"Maybe we can pick up the tracks farther away from camp," Orville suggested.

"Yeah," Agatha agreed. "Let's try that way. Away from the rest of the searchers."

But all they found were hiking boot tracks that fell in the average size range. Nothing close to a sixteen.

No other clues either. Nothing but dirt and trees and lake water.

Orville's watch beeped. "If we are going to be back at the tent on time, we have to turn around."

"Then we better turn around. I don't want to have to watch Mildred go into a tizzy tailspin," Agatha said. They returned at the exact moment the half hour was up. Everyone else was already at the meeting place.

"Any luck?" Mildred asked.

Orville found the concept of luck to be incomprehensible. Agatha had tried to explain it to him many times, but it had never made sense. So he didn't answer the head counselor.

"No Stu," Agatha said. Orville didn't see what that had to do with Mildred's question about luck, but the counselor nodded.

"So . . . teachers or no teachers?" Clark asked softly.

Mildred shifted her weight from one foot to the other. "Having a camper snatched on your watch is very serious. It might even affect *me*—even though I certainly wasn't in charge of your tent. I wonder if my trip to Yellowstone would get taken away. . . ."

"I guess I would have no chance of being head counselor next year if this came out," Clark said.

Mildred just snorted in reply.

"But if Stu really was really snatched by Ax Jack—or even just somebody who thinks he's Ax Jack," Adam said, "isn't he gonna get . . . you know . . ." Adam mimed swooshing an ax through the air.

"Not right away," Mike reminded him. "The vitamin thing, remember? Ax Jack makes his victims eat those minerals for two days before he . . . you know. . . ."

"I think Agatha's right about Stu being a jerk and playing some ridiculous joke," Clark said. "He lives to torture me."

"Orville and I can definitely find the little rat boy," Agatha said. "We have a one hundred percent success rate."

Orville didn't think two cases were enough data on

which to make statistical evaluations, but he didn't say anything.

"Let them do it," Adam said. "Otherwise, the teachers will send us all home. The camping trip will be ruined for everyone."

Clark and Mildred stared at each other. "Do you all agree to keep this a secret?" Mildred finally asked the group of kids huddled near the grills.

She got nods and yeahs from everybody.

"Okay," Mildred said. "But one, I have to remind you all that Stu was taken from the boys' tent, not mine. And two—" She turned to Orville and Agatha. "You have until the end of the day today to find him. That's all. Once the sun goes down, we tell the teachers."

"No problem," Agatha said. "We'll find Stu by lunchtime. Guaranteed!" She turned to Orville. "Come on. Let's do the strategy thing." She led the way to a long rock next to the cold fire pit.

"What if Stu's not playing a trick?" Orville asked. "What if you're wrong and he's in trouble?"

Agatha's eyes widened. "That's not possible . . . is it?"

"Yes," Orville answered. He couldn't calculate the exact percentage of the chance that Stu was in danger. But it was definitely possible.

Agatha gulped.

Chapter 2

"Left, right, left, right. Stay with your buddy. And march, march, march!" Ms. Winogrand called out.

"If the search for Stu is our top priority, we should have begun as soon as we got dressed," Orville pointed out as he and Agatha followed the others down a wide, dusty path.

"Ssh!" she hissed. "Ixnay on the Ustay."

Pig Latin, Orville thought. Agatha had taught it to him in third grade. He instantly translated the phrase. "Nix on the Stu."

"Aargh!" Agatha cried. "Don't say his name. We can't let any of the bigwigs realize that he's missing, remember?"

Orville looked around. "Unless one of the teachers has extremely fine-tuned hearing, we are out of range," he told her. His breathing rate had increased since he'd left the campsite. Ms. Winogrand had set a marching pace of approximately two hundred and nine steps per minute.

"It *would* have been better to start the search right away," Agatha said. "But Mildred was afraid that if we left before breakfast, one of the teachers would get suspicious. It's easier to cover up one missing kid at the morning head count than three."

"Why are we doing a hike before the hike?" Vanessa Morrisey complained.

"It's a warm-up! Everyone knows you need to warm up before you go on a hike!" Ms. Winogrand answered, gasping for breath every third word. She began marching faster. "Left, right, left, right, left, right."

"But if it's a warm-up, shouldn't we be going slower?" Adam called from farther back in the line. "I think I'm getting a cramp."

"The pace is appropriate." Ms. Winogrand began to cough as she turned and marched backward for a few steps, surveying the line of kids. "I. Will. Have. No. Stragglers."

"Ms. Wino is such a koo-koo," Agatha complained. "She had us all in marching formation before the oatmeal had gotten from my mouth to my belly."

Orville found that unlikely. For one thing, each bite of the oatmeal made its way individually from mouth to stomach. So at least a small percentage of the oatmeal would have made it to Agatha's belly by this time.

"But you're right. We're losing daylight," Agatha went on. "We'll never find Stu if we don't even start looking. I'll come up with a plan to get out of the big hike. Then the Ustay hunt can begin."

"Left, right, left, right. And halt!" Ms. Winogrand shouted.

Agatha snorted. "Unbelievable. She hiked us to the Quick-E-Mart."

Orville looked around. They were near the entrance to South Haven Park. The blue-and-orange neon sign over the door to the little store plainly stated that this was indeed a Quick-E-Mart. "It is highly believable that she hiked us to the Quick-E-Mart," he told Agatha. "If you observe—"

"I mean, I can't believe she made us come here," Agatha explained. "We're supposed to be on a camping trip, soaking in nature." She stared around at the SUVs and RVs in the small parking lot. "I hate it when vehicles are taller than I am," she muttered.

"Ten-minute rest break." Ms. Winogrand pulled in a deep, shuddering breath. "Then we hike back to the campsite. I will be calling roll before the return hike. Do. Not. Be. Late." Ms. Wino disappeared into the Quick-E-Mart as soon as the last word was out of her purple-lipsticked mouth.

"Rest break, my little toe. She's sick of the great outdoors already." Agatha shook her head. "Well, since we're here, I am in dire need of peanuts. I can't work on the you-know-what without peanuts. Because peanuts are brain food, according to my nana. And the you-know-what is all about having the noggin in top shape."

Orville thought his brain worked fine on his usual breakfast of one hard-boiled egg, one apple, and one Kraft Single slice of American cheese. He'd been able to bring all of these items with him to camp and had already consumed them while the others were eating oatmeal cooked over the campfire.

Clearly the oatmeal hadn't satisfied everyone, because what Orville estimated to be fifty-three percent of the campers were already in the store when he and Agatha entered. Rachel Loiacono and Mike Iburg were fighting over the last package of strawberry licorice, which Orville thought tasted absolutely nothing like strawberries. Adam was buying cream cheese and crackers. Ms. Winogrand had an entire basket full of Sno Balls and the new issue of *Motor Trend* magazine. And Clark was loaded down with a plastic container of rainbow sprinkles, a bag of marshmallows, and a bag of Cheez Doodles.

"Do you have pearl onions?" Clark called to the teenage cashier. "I need pearl onions!"

"I don't even know what a pearl onion is," the cashier answered.

"It's a little white . . . onion. That's pickled or something. It's in a bottle."

"Pearl onions are produced from the bulblets of the species *Allium cepa*," Orville added helpfully. "Or *Allium ampeloprasum* L. var. *sectivum*, which is often considered a pearl onion too."

Clark, Agatha, and the cashier stared blankly at him for 2.5 seconds.

"Maybe try an olive," a woman with a baby strapped to her back suggested.

"Hey, why are you buying the stuff for Stu's repulsivo trail mix?" Agatha asked Clark.

"It's *my* repulsivo trail mix, actually," Clark answered. "I'm the one who taught Stu the recipe."

"Stu told us it was *his* recipe," Orville replied.

"Typical." Clark rolled his eyes. "He takes credit for everything." He frowned. "Though I hope we get him back soon. I kind of miss him."

"Yeah." Agatha's cheeks had grown fifteen percent redder than usual. "Uh . . . we miss him too."

Orville thought she was lying. The combination of red cheeks and slight tremble in her voice was usually a sign that Agatha wasn't telling the truth. He had been learning to look for those signs, because Agatha didn't like it when he told people that she was lying. But he didn't have enough data yet to be sure that he could accurately tell Lying Agatha apart from Embarrassed Agatha or Angry Agatha. The physical symptoms were remarkably similar.

"Are you lying?" he asked.

"No!" Agatha and Clark both cried.

"Look, we need a plan," Clark said. "I may not like Stu very much, but he *is* my cousin. And I'm gonna get in big trouble if we don't find him." He grabbed a bottle of green olives and headed for the cash register. Agatha followed, snatching a bag of peanuts on the way.

"Don't worry. We'll totally find him today," Agatha told Clark. "I'm sure—" She hesitated, shooting a glance at Orville. "I'm *pretty* sure that he's found himself a comfy little hiding place. We just have to track him down like a dog."

Clark and Agatha paid. "Okay, time for that plan," Agatha said. "Follow me." She walked over to a picnic table outside the Quick-E-Mart and sat down. "Orville, map."

Orville pulled the map of South Haven Park from the back pocket of his pants. He had sent away for it as soon as the camping trip had been announced. His mother had thought that he would feel less anxious about the trip if he could memorize the layout of the park in advance. He wasn't sure if it had worked or not, because he had no way of knowing how anxious he would have been if he had not studied the map.

"We need to find the places in the park that would make good Stu hideouts," Agatha announced.

"How are we supposed to figure that out?" Clark asked. He took the trail mix ingredients out of a Quick-E-Mart bag.

"Clues. And logic. And . . . clues. That's what makes us detectives," Agatha said.

"O-kay," Clark mumbled. He poured all the mini-marshmallows into the bag, followed by the rainbow sprinkles.

"Orville, what would you want in a hiding place?" Agatha asked.

"Water," Orville said. "Water is necessary for regulating body temperature, nutrient metabolism, and cushioning joints, organs, and tissues."

"So we need to look for places near water." Agatha looked over Orville's shoulder as he opened the map. "And the place can't be anywhere near where the group is supposed to hike—Stu wouldn't want anyone to spot him."

Clark opened the Cheez Doodles and began to pour them into the Quick-E-Mart bag.

Orville stared at the orange puffs falling into the plastic bag. Clark was putting way too many doodles into the trail mix. "The ratio of Cheez Doodles to marshmallows is three to ten," he said.

"Huh?"

"You put in too many doodles," Agatha told Clark.

"Stu gave out the recipe?" Clark asked.

"No," Orville said.

"Orville notices everything," Agatha explained. "That's what makes him a fabulosa detective."

Orville pointed to the map. "Dead Man's Ditch would make a good hiding place. There's a creek nearby. And it's unlikely that anyone would hike in the ditch. The closest hiking trail is on the other side of the creek."

"That place is haunted!" Clark cried.

"Plus it's a three-hour hike from here," Agatha said, ignoring him. "Is there anyplace closer?"

Orville studied the map. "There's an abandoned farm. There's a creek near it, too."

"Snakes always move into places that are abandoned," Clark whined.

Agatha rolled her eyes. "The farm sounds like a good starting place to me." She traced a thin blue line on the map. "We can follow this little trail. It shouldn't take more than a half hour or so." Agatha began stuffing the map in her backpack.

Orville managed to snatch a corner of the map before Agatha got it completely inside her pack. "We have exactly twenty seconds until Ms. Winogrand's roll call," he said. Luckily, it only took twelve seconds to properly refold the map. Orville had done it many times before. "Then we hike back to the campsite. And then the nature hike begins."

"Wait a minute," Clark said. "How are you going to find Stu when you have to spend all morning hiking?"

"We'll skip the hike," Agatha said.

"But the entire class is required to go on the nature hike," Orville pointed out. "We can't skip it."

"Orville, we're not going on the hike," Agatha said. "We have to search for Stu."

"The hike is a requirement," Orville answered. His

heart rate sped up slightly. He must be getting anxious. He became anxious whenever he broke a rule.

"Finding Stu is the top priority, remember?" Clark said. "I'll come with you guys."

"We don't need any help," Agatha said.

"I know, but he's my cousin. I want to help," Clark replied.

"Fine," Agatha answered.

But it wasn't fine. "The hike is a req—" Orville began.

"Clark is your counselor, right?" Agatha interrupted.

"Yes," Orville said.

"And you are supposed to do what he says, right?" Agatha asked.

"Yes," Orville said.

Agatha turned to Clark. "Please tell Orville that he doesn't have to go on the hike."

"You don't have to go on the hike, Orville," Clark told him.

Orville nodded. Clark shook some olives into the trail mix.

"There are quite a lot of pearl onions in Stu's trail mix," Orville said. "One onion for every two marshmallows."

"Oh." Clark frowned. "I don't like olives as much as onions, though. I'm not sure I should put as many in." He gave the bag a shake to mix the ingredients. "I gotta hit the bathroom before we head back to camp. See you guys in a second."

Agatha chewed on her lip for a moment. "Now we just need to find a way to escape from the group. You play along."

"How?"

"You'll know when the time is right," Agatha said, her voice seven percent deeper than usual. Orville suspected she was trying to be mysterious.

Chapter 3

"You don't feel feverish to me," Ms. Winogramd said, wearing a suspicious-house-cat-being-given-new-cat-food expression. A bright pink Sno Ball crumb hung from one corner of her mouth. She moved her clammy hand from Agatha's forehead to her cheek.

Agatha bit her lip, forcing herself to endure the torture of the Wino temperature touch. "I never get fevers," she lied. "It's a rare genetic trait. No one in my family has a temperature above ninety-two degrees. When I get up to normal, it means I'm deathly ill. It's like the equivalent of a hundred-and-four fever or something."

Orville frowned. "A body temperature of ninety-two degrees would be—"

"Shocking. I know," Agatha interrupted him. Orville had a bad habit of correcting her outlandish stories at the worst possible time. "But that's the Wong way."

Ms. Winograd finally removed her hand. "You say your stomach hurts?"

"Yeah," Agatha said. "Big time. I might vomit at any moment." She gave a little lurch for effect. Ms. Wino jumped away, her eyes going wide with alarm. "I think it's a virus," Agatha added. "I'm probably highly contagious."

Ms. Winogrand reached for the flap of her tent, and Agatha wondered if she was just going to bolt. "You shouldn't hike, then," Ms. Wino said. "We mustn't risk getting the other children sick. You . . . you can just stay in your tent."

Agatha sucked in her cheeks a little to make herself look gaunt. "All alone?" she whispered.

"Oh." Ms. Wino's expression changed to terrified-dog-being-dragged-to-bathtub. "I suppose I *can't* leave you alone."

"I'm sure one of the counselors would stay with me," Agatha said. "Maybe Clark Frysley?"

It was a tactical error. Ms. Wino's eyes narrowed. "Clark is a *boys'* counselor," she said. "Boys are not allowed in the girls' tents," Orville put in. "So technically, Clark can't keep you company."

Think fast, Agatha ordered herself. "I was only thinking of Orville's welfare," she told Ms. Wino. "He's sick too. And Clark's the counselor for his tent."

"I'm not sick," Orville said.

"Not *yet*," Agatha agreed. "But I've been hanging out with Orville all morning, Ms. Winogrand, and all day yesterday. It's only a matter of time before he gets vomitous too." She leaned closer to the teacher. "And when Orville is sick, it's not pretty."

Ms. Winogrand shot a look at Orville, who stared calmly back at her. "What do you mean?" she murmured.

"Let's just say he's not a good patient," Agatha told her, trying to make it sound meaningful. In reality, sick Orville behaved exactly the same as healthy Orville, but Ms. Wino didn't need to know that. "I think we'd both be better off with a counselor who can deal with Orville."

Ms. Winogrand's face scrunched up like a shrunken-apple doll.

"Since you decided Orville and I both need to skip the hike, it would be better if Clark stayed with us," Agatha pressed on.

Baby-tasting-mashed-Brussels-sprouts, Agatha thought as she watched Ms. Wino's face change expressions. *Or maybe groundhog-seeing-shadow.*

"Clark . . . Frysley," Ms. Winogrand said slowly.

Agatha nodded. "That's who you suggested."

"Actually," Orville began, "it was *you* who—"

Agatha took a huge breath and launched into the world's loudest fake coughing fit. As she coughed, she watched Orville's mouth move. She just hoped Ms. Wino couldn't hear him over all the racket.

"Unless you want to put Mildred in charge," Agatha said, when Orville's mouth finally stopped moving and she could stop coughing. "In fact, I think I'd feel more comfortable with—"

"No, no!" Ms. Winogrand interrupted. "I said you're staying with Clark Frysley and that's final."

"Well, okay," Agatha said. "You're doing the right

thing, Ms. Winogrand. Orville and I really shouldn't be around the other campers."

"Precisely." Ms. Winogrand cleared her throat. "That's what I've been saying all along."

"Yes," Agatha said, clutching her stomach.

"I'll find Mr. Frysley and send him in," Ms. Wino said. "You two feel better."

"Your shoes are brown," Orville told her.

Ms. Wino looked ready to cry. "Excuse me?"

"Your shoes are brown," Orville repeated.

"I think it's a compliment," Agatha explained.

"Oh." Ms. Wino opened her mouth, then closed it again. Goldfish-in-glass-bowl. Agatha had a hard time keeping a straight face. "Oh," Ms. Wino added. Then she fled from the tent.

Clark showed up two minutes later. "How did you guys do that?" he asked. "Ms. Winogrand practically ordered me to skip the hike."

Agatha shrugged. "I keep telling you, we're good."

Clark pulled back the flap and peered outside. "Okay, everyone else is leaving," he said. "Let's go."

Agatha slipped through the tent flap and hurried toward the edge of the campsite. The others had taken the main trail north, but she and Orville and Clark had to head west. "The little trail should be over behind the barbecue pit," she said. It wasn't hard to find. Agatha pulled her backpack up higher on her shoulders, and together she, Orville, and Clark set off to find Stu.

The trail quickly dwindled to a footpath. The enormous pine trees were pushing in on both sides, like they were trying to block the path with their branches. The scratchy needles brushed against Agatha's face and bare arms as they walked in silence.

Clark sneezed. "Shouldn't we be looking for footprints?" he asked.

"Eighty-three percent of detective shows on television have used the footprint as a vital clue at least once," Orville added.

The sun was high in the sky, but the pines were close together, and they blocked out a lot of the golden rays. Weeds and dead pine needles covered the ground. It wasn't exactly a footprint-friendly location.

"We don't need any stinking footprints," Agatha said. "We have something more important: a psychological profile." She grinned. That sounded important. It was amazing how much she'd learned in only two cases as a detective. "We know that Stu, being Stu, would want the most comfortable hideout he could find."

"Seventy-one percent of detective shows on television have used the psychological profile as a vital clue," Orville said.

Clark sneezed again.

"Your sneezing is extremely loud," Orville complimented him.

"I think my allergies are acting up," Clark complained. "How long until we reach the farm thing?"

A long howl split the air.

Agatha jumped, startled.

Another howl rang out, joining in with the first one. Clark's face went pale. Agatha's heart pounded against her ribs. Those were wolf howls. From real, live wolves.

"At our current rate, we should be at the farm in another five minutes," Orville said.

Leave it to my best friend to totally ignore a wolf, Agatha thought. Orville sounded so normal that she began to feel silly for being spooked. She shook it off and forced her mind back to the Stu search.

A third howl split the air.

It was joined by a low whine—from Clark.

Agatha hated to admit that Stu could be right about anything. But his cousin did seem to be kind of a chicken.

"I don't see the trail anymore," Orville announced.

"It's right there." Agatha pointed to a space between two trees. Then she frowned. That space looked kind of like a . . . space. Not like a trail. Or even a path. She turned to the right and studied the forest on that side. Lots of spaces between trees. No path.

More howls broke out.

"The map shows this trail leading straight to the farm," Orville said. His voice sounded the same as always, but Agatha knew he was getting anxious. Maps were supposed

to be correct. If they weren't, Orville freaked. There was
only one thing to do: distract him again.

"Come on," she said cheerfully, squeezing between
the two trees. "We'll just keep going in this direction
and the path will probably reappear."

"Are you insane?" Clark cried. "Those are wolves!"

Agatha turned to him and put her hands on her hips.
"We're in the woods. Of course there are going to be . . .
animals. Is that going to make you give up looking for Stu?"

Clark hesitated. Then he shook his head.

"All right, then. Left, right, left, right," Agatha said.
She picked her way through the forest, trying to walk in
a straight line but weaving around trees when she had
to. A little voice in her head started talking to her.
Wolves, wolves, it squeaked. *There are wolves out here,
Agatha. WOLVES! What are you doing? Wol-ves.* She
tried to ignore the voice. But it was hard. Because the
wolves kept howling.

"They're getting closer," Clark muttered.

"I believe we are getting closer to them," Orville suggested. "I think they have remained almost stationary."

"Hey! Look up over those two trees," Clark said. "Is
that smoke?"

"Yes," Orville said. "We've been getting closer to
that too."

"And you didn't tell us? How long have you been
seeing that smoke?" she asked him.

"I first noticed it five-point-two minutes ago," he said.

"Why didn't you say something?" Clark cried.

"Because we didn't ask," Agatha replied quickly. One thing she'd learned from solving mysteries with Orville was that he didn't volunteer information. On the plus side, he noticed *everything*. But on the minus side, he couldn't tell which info was vital and which info was useless. It was her job to get the important stuff out of Orville's spongelike brain, and obviously she'd been shirking her duty as the less-brilliant-but-more-intuitive member of the team.

"That looks like smoke from a chimney," she told Orville. "Maybe our abandoned farm isn't so abandoned. Maybe it's inhabited by one Stu Frysley. Let's check it out."

"We need to adjust our course point-zero-zero-two degrees to the northwest."

Agatha turned ever so slightly left and started pushing her way through the trees. *No, no, no!* the little voice in her head protested. *Don't go toward the wolves. That's stupid. That's how you get your face eaten off.* Agatha ignored the voice. And the trickle of sweat sliding down her back.

The wolves howled, the sounds growing closer . . . closer . . . until they were all Agatha could hear. She pushed aside one final tree branch . . .

And caught her breath in horror.

The wolves were *everywhere*! There had to be at least fifteen of them, and they were all looking at her with their wild yellow eyes. One of the wolves stepped forward and let out a low growl. It pulled back its upper lip, revealing a row of jagged teeth.

Clark stepped up behind her. "They're in pens," he whispered.

Agatha nodded. Chain-link pens surrounded the tiny cabin on all sides. Each pen had a fence about eight feet high and eight feet wide. And each pen had a giant wolf in it. And each wolf was staring at Agatha, Orville, and Clark as if they were a delicious meal about to be served.

Shake it off, Agatha told herself. *The wolves are in cages. What matters is the cabin.* "We have to get a look inside," she said aloud. "It's not the farm, but Stu couldn't ask for a better hideout. Do you think he could have talked whoever lives there into letting him stay for a little while?"

"We can't go in there," Clark whispered.

"Why not?" Agatha asked.

"There are wolves."

"In cages," Agatha answered. "Should we just knock on the door?"

"There's no one home," Orville put in.

"How do you know there's nobody home?" Clark asked.

"Because the smoke coming from that chimney has been dwindling at a steady rate ever since I first noticed it," Orville said.

Agatha grinned at Clark's confused-puppy expression. "Why is that important, Orville?" she asked—solely for Clark's benefit.

"At the rate the smoke is diminishing, the fire inside will most likely go out within ten minutes. It is likely—although not definitely true—that if someone were inside, they would tend the fire to keep it from going out," Orville explained. "Combined with the fact that the wolves have been howling for seven minutes straight *and* the fact that no one has noticed us standing here, I estimate a ninety-eight percent chance that we'll find the cabin unoccupied."

"I want to check it out. If Stu was ever inside, we should be able to find some clues. Follow me," Agatha said, and took off across the dead leaves and pine needles that covered the clearing around the cabin. The wolves howled louder and turned in their pens to keep an eye on her.

They can't hurt you; they're in cages, she told herself over and over as she ran toward the cabin. She was a big fan of dogs—in fact, she'd been nagging her parents to get her a cute, cute Chesapeake Bay retriever for the last two years—but these were wild animals. They might have looked like a cross between Lassie and the Tramp, but their eyes were cold.

Curtains covered the two small windows in the front of the cabin. Cursed curtains. Agatha reached the front door, grabbed the handle, and yanked, all without pausing.

Nothing happened.

She yanked again.

"Come on, hurry!" Clark urged.

"It's locked," Agatha said. She tried one more time. The door didn't budge.

"Bummer. Well, let's go." Clark turned and began scurrying back toward the trees.

"Hey! Hold on," Agatha yelled. "We're not through yet!" She edged her way around the cabin, following a path worn in the grass between the building and the nearest wolf pens. The space was only about three feet wide. The wolves pressed up against the chain-link fences, growling.

"What are you looking for?" Orville asked as he followed her.

Agatha bit her lip. "I'll know it when I see it," she told him. Then she glanced up at the wall of the cabin. "There it is!"

Orville peered up at a half-open window near the roof of the small building.

"We can't fit through there," Clark said from behind Orville.

It *did* look pretty small. Still, Agatha had a feeling that it was their only way in. "You can't, but I might," she said. "Help me. I need a boost."

"This is crazy!" Clark cried. "That window is, like, ten inches wide."

"It is at least twenty inches wide," Orville corrected him. "And Agatha is surprisingly small."

"Thanks for the compliment," she said. "Clark, boost me up."

"Was that a compliment?" Orville asked.

Clark knelt down and made a cradle with his hands. Agatha stuck her Converse into it and he lifted her until she could grab the bottom of the window.

"Hurry, okay? This is trespassing," Clark said as she pulled herself up and inside. She swung her legs over the sill and dropped to the floor of the cabin. She landed in a crouch—

Right in front of the wolf.

This one wasn't in a cage. Its snout was half an inch away from her nose. She could feel its hot breath on her face. She could feel something under her hands, too. Something hard and crunchy. She glanced down.

Oh, no! She'd landed right on the wolf's gigantic bowl of food. That was extreme badness. Now she would smell like din-din to the wolf. The wolf let out a low growl. Agatha forced herself to look at it. The beast bared its teeth. Its *big* teeth.

She slowly began to back away, still on all fours.

And the wolf pounced.

Chapter 4

"Agatha?" Orville called. "Why are you screaming?"

"There's something in there," Clark said. Orville noticed he was sweating, which made no sense because it was only 70.3 degrees out. "She needs help! I'll go find some!" Clark turned and ran off.

"Agatha?" Orville called again.

"Nice wolfie," Agatha's voice came from inside. "Good wolfie." She was speaking at an extremely slow rate—generally Agatha's words had less than a twentieth of a second in between them—and her voice was seventy percent higher pitched than usual, which meant she was extremely agitated.

"Ummm . . . Orville? I could use a little help in here." Apparently Clark was right. Agatha needed him. But he couldn't even see her. He needed to get up to the height of the window. But how?

Orville glanced around. He turned to the wolf pen right behind him. A wolf stared at him from the other side of the chain-link fence.

Chain-link fence.

Orville hesitated. He had never climbed a fence before, but he'd seen other kids do it. They just stuck their feet in the holes and pulled themselves up. But Orville could never get his body to do what he wanted it to do. No matter how hard he tried, he was clumsy. Miss Eloise, his social skills teacher, said it was because of his Asperger's syndrome.

But Agatha was in trouble. And she was his best friend. She would have tried to save him. And he was going to try to save her.

He reached for the fence. If he could climb two feet up the fence, he would be able to see in the window. Two feet wasn't very high.

The first step is to find footholds at least six inches high, he thought. He stuck his black shoe toward a hole. The shoe was too wide to fit in.

Orville pulled his shoes off.

He stuck his sock into the hole in the fence. The wolf in the pen stared at the 3.8 centimeters of sock-covered toe that protruded into its territory. Would he try to bite it? Orville tried to calculate the probability, then realized it didn't matter. *Agatha needs me*, he told himself. Whatever the probability, he had to take the chance.

Orville reached up and grabbed onto another hole. He pulled his weight up and aimed his other foot at the fence. He missed.

He tried again and managed to get his foot into a hole. Just one more step up and he would be there!

A growl drifted through the window.

"Agatha?" he called. "What's going on?"

"A wolf-ie has me cor-nered!" she called back, half singing and half talking. "Every time I try to mo-ove, he ju-umps at me!"

Orville's heart gave a lurch, as if it had skipped a beat. He must be frightened. The key to overcoming fear was to keep thinking logically. So if Agatha was trapped in a cabin with a wolf, there were several ways to help her. One could subdue the wolf with a sedative of some kind. Generally animals were shot with tran-quilizer darts, he believed. Or one could trap the wolf under a net by dropping the net from above. One could also lure the animal away from Agatha with a piece of meat or other food product and then trap it in a cage.

"Orville, help!" Agatha called.

He didn't have tranquilizer darts, or a net, or any food products. But he had to do something. Orville let go of the fence and threw his body toward the window. His fingers caught the lip of the windowsill, and his socks slammed into the wall of the cabin. Orville squished his toes against the wall and pushed up until he got his arms over the windowsill. Inside he could see Agatha in the corner. He had to get to her.

He pulled himself up as hard as he could and fell through the window to the floor below. "Orville!" Agatha cried. "What are you doing?"

"Helping you," he answered.

"Helping me?" Agatha cried. "Now we're both trapped!"

The big wolf spun and charged at Orville.

"Grandma, sit!" a voice ordered.

Agatha blinked as the wolf immediately plopped its butt on the ground. That woman had some powerful mojo!

"Good girl." The woman who'd just come in grabbed the wolf behind its ears and kissed it on the head. "You're such a fierce beast," she added cheerfully.

The wolf whined and dropped to the floor, rolling over to have its stomach rubbed.

Maybe the wolf attacked me and knocked me unconscious and I'm dreaming all this, Agatha thought. Between Orville climbing through a window and the wolf acting like somebody's pet beagle, she had to be in a dream state.

Clark stuck his head through the cabin door. "Is it safe now?"

"Sure." The woman waved him in. "Grandma's a big softie. I've had her since she was two weeks old."

"Um . . ." Agatha shook her head. She couldn't think of a thing to say, and that was definitely a sign that something was wrong. "Um . . ."

"I'm Willa Myer," the woman said. "I'm with the rangers here."

"Oh. Hi." Agatha shot a glance at Orville. He was

still sitting on the floor. "Uh, why was your wolf—why was Grandma attacking us?"

"She wasn't," Willa said. "She was just guarding you. You know, keeping you in place until I could get home and decide what to do with you. She'd never actually bite you or anything. But she looks pretty scary if she wants to."

"Grandma has big teeth," Orville commented, in compliment mode.

"I'll say." Clark sank into one of the two chairs in the tiny room. "I thought Agatha would be eaten by the time we got back."

"You went to get help?" Agatha asked. "Thanks."

"Well, I couldn't lose *two* campers on my watch," he said with a grin. "Although I guess you weren't in as much trouble as I thought."

"Wait. Orville, how did you even get up to the window without a boost?" Agatha asked.

"I climbed up the fence and then jumped," Orville answered calmly. Like it was no biggie. Like doing anything that physical wasn't a huge challenge for him.

"That's so incredible," Agatha said. "Thanks a ga-whatever is higher than a trillion."

"You're welcome," Orville said carefully.

Agatha smiled. Orville had learned about the thank-you-you're-welcome deal in his social skills class a few years back.

"So let's hear it," Willa said. "What are you kids

doing in my cabin? You're upsetting the wolves—and Grandma's the only tame one—not to mention breaking and entering."

Agatha bit her lip. Breaking and entering was not good. Nana wouldn't want to hear those words in the same sentence with the name "Agatha."

"We were looking for someone," Clark started to explain.

Agatha interrupted so that Clark wouldn't go blabbing about Stu and getting them all in trouble. She talked very fast so that Orville wouldn't have the chance to interrupt—with the truth.

"We were looking for someone who lives in a cabin in the park," Agatha told Willa. "We thought your cabin was their cabin, and since we're friends, we didn't think they'd mind if we climbed in the window. Then I got the Grandma welcome. Yikes."

Willa looked ready to ask some questions, so Agatha decided to beat her to it. "Why do you have her and all the other wolves anyway?"

"The wolves are going to be reintroduced to their natural habitat here in the park. They've been raised in captivity but kept away from human interaction. In other words, they learned to hunt on the preserve where they lived. Now we're going to release them here and hope they do the same thing. It's a move to keep them from becoming extinct."

"So you're a wolf scientist or something?" Clark said. "Cool!"

"Not really. I'm just a park ranger with some training in zoology. I'm the one who will be keeping tabs on the wolves here at South Haven." Willa pushed her long, dark bangs off her forehead. "The 'wolf scientists' check in every month."

"Great!" Agatha said. "Cool. Awe-inspiring."

Willa's walkie-talkie gave a burst of static. "Oops," she said. "Time for me to get back on patrol. Everybody out now."

She ushered them from the cabin, locked the door, and headed off on her ATV with a wave.

"Well, it's almost lunchtime. We have to head back to the campgrounds or we'll get caught," Clark said. "Too bad this was such a dead end."

"We can at least go back to that little trail and try another direction from the end of it," Agatha argued. "We only came this way because we saw the smoke. We still have to find the abandoned farm."

"No way. We have to go back. Come on." Clark turned and headed straight for the trees. Straight back where they'd come from. Agatha hated to give up on the case. She wasn't a quitter. And what about Stu?

"Clark is our counselor," Orville told her. "We have to do what he says."

So Agatha tromped back to the woods after Clark. "I

couldn't believe it when Willa and I came into the cabin and I saw you in there," Clark said to Orville. "You really didn't know that wolf was tame before you went in?"

"No. It was the wrong angle to see its collar," Orville replied.

Clark shook his head. "And I turned around and ran."

"You ran for help," Orville reminded him.

"Yeah, but still . . ." Clark frowned. "How did you do it? Really? You've got to tell me. You had to be scared."

Agatha looked at Orville. She wanted to hear the answer to that question too.

"My heartbeat became erratic, so I knew I was frightened. But I also knew that Agatha needed me. I decided the way through the fear was to think logically," Orville explained. "So I thought of the ways that I could help Agatha rather than thinking about the wolf."

Agatha's insides turned to warm marshmallow goo. She wanted to give Orville a great big rib-buster hug. But that would be exactly the wrong way to show him how much of an *Oprah* moment he had just given her. "You're the best friend I could possibly have," she told him instead.

"Yeah, you really are a good friend," Clark said. "I can't believe you'd put yourself in danger like that."

Agatha glared at him. How could Clark be all impressed with Orville but still want to give up on the search for his own cousin? Wasn't he worried about Stu? If she'd decided to give up, that would have been one thing. After all, Stu Frysley was her sworn enemy for all eternity. But Clark was his family! Wasn't he supposed to love Stu? Well, maybe not *love* him, because Agatha wasn't sure it was possible to love the little wiener. But Clark should at least have been concerned about his cousin. Was he just so afraid that all he cared about was getting back to the safety of the camp? He had seemed poised of the brink of a freak-out all day. But if Agatha had been missing, she knew that all her cousins would have been out combing the woods for her, even the ones who didn't appreciate her the way they should.

A sharp sound caught Agatha's attention. Clark was snapping his fingers in her face.

"What?" she asked.

"You were zoning out," Orville explained. "I tried to snap my fingers to get you out of it, but I can't do it. Clark can."

"Oh." Agatha felt a blush creep up her cheeks. Zoning out was Orville's bag, not hers. But the unsolved Stu-snatcher case had her acting weird. "What's up?"

"I think we're lost," Clark said.

"How could we be lost? We just had to follow that same path," Agatha answered.

"We haven't been following the same path," Orville told her.

"We haven't?" Clark burst out.

"Well, that explains the lostness. Can you figure out where we are on the map?" she asked Orville.

Orville pulled the map out of his pocket and carefully unfolded it.

"I wish I hadn't eaten all of my peanuts in the parking lot of the Quick-E-Mart," Agatha said. "Meeting Grandma gave me an appetite. I think I could even eat some of your trail mix of repulsiveness, Clark."

"Ate it all. Sorry," he said.

"There are wild blueberries," Orville said, pointing to a plant near the edge of the little trail.

"Wait a minute," Clark said. "Look into the trees— do you see a drop-off?"

"Uh-huh," Agatha said.

"Would you call it a ravine?" Clark asked.

Orville peered through the trees. "Yes."

"Um, you guys, blueberries, plus a ravine, plus we're in an area where wolves live. Does that mean anything to you?" Clark's voice was shaking. "He's friends with wolves," Clark continued. "He drinks blueberry-and-blood milk shakes. He dumps the bodies of his victims in a ravine."

The little hairs on the back of Agatha's neck stood on end. "Are you saying you think Ax Jack is real?"

Chapter 5

"I'm saying that Ax Jack is real and that he's somewhere right around here!" Clark exclaimed. "We've gotta get—"

"Wait, wait. It's impossible," Agatha interrupted him. "I mean, Ax Jack—who has a name like that? He's just a legend, like the Creature from the Black Lagoon or the Headless Horseman. Or Trixie!"

"I believe—" Orville began.

"And we've been hearing Ax Jack stories since we were like five," Agatha went on. "My cousin Preston used to chase me with a plastic ax whenever I went over to his house. So there can't be a real Ax Jack, because if he were real, they wouldn't talk about him to five-year-olds. Nobody would tell a little kid about a *real* killer. He's totally not real. Right?"

The only answer was a moan. A low, deep sound that made her bones rattle. Agatha shivered.

"That's the voices of Ax Jack's victims moaning!" Clark cried.

"If there were actual victims, I don't believe their larynxes could survive the dismemberment. Nor could the voices sound without the brain sending—"

"He meant the *ghosts* of his victims," Agatha clarified. "It can't be ghost voices, right?"

Orville just blinked at her. She got the feeling that he was offended by the question. Or maybe just baffled by it. It was hard to tell with him sometimes. "The wind, tunneled through the narrow ravine, creates a sound like moaning," Orville told Agatha and Clark.

"Why didn't you just say that's what it was?" Agatha asked her best friend.

"I *did* just say that's what it was," Orville replied.

"Come on, let's look at the map and figure out how to get back to the camp," Clark said. "If Ms. Wino finds us gone, she'll flip her wig."

"What purpose would that serve?" Orville asked.

"It's just an expression, Orville," Agatha told him. "Although in Wino's case there might actually be a wig involved."

"What I mean is that we'll get in trouble. Big trouble." Clark frowned. "I'm pretty sure I already lost my shot at head counselor. But if I get caught sneaking around in the woods with two sick campers, I'll *definitely* lose it."

Agatha glared at Clark. "If there is an Ax Jack—and I'm not saying there is—but if there is, maybe he really did take Stu. We have to look for him."

Clark shifted from foot to foot.

"You're the one who made the connection," Agatha reminded him. "We've got blueberries, a ravine, and moaning sounds. We've got an area where wolves live."

"And a hidden path through the woods," Orville added. He pointed to a thin line of dirt that snaked into the forest along the rim of the ravine.

Agatha's mouth dropped open. It *was* a path. How could she not have seen it?

"That's not a path," Clark said.

"It is too." Agatha took off, following the narrow course. It wasn't easy. The pathway wasn't marked, and it wasn't obvious. But the underbrush had been worn away in a definite line, and the dirt underneath showed through. She'd only gone about five feet when she decided to put the maestro front and center. "Orville, you go first," she said. "You can see the path better than me."

"I said, it's not a path," Clark insisted from behind them, his voice going high and squeaky. "We're going back to camp."

"You can go back to camp. Orville and I are going to find Stu," Agatha said.

"I forbid you to follow that path!" Clark cried. But it sounded more like begging than forbidding. "Not that it's a path in the first place."

"It turns up here," Orville called from about fifteen

feet away. Agatha hurried after him, Clark following. Sure enough, the line of dirt veered to the left, then skirted the end of the ravine. On the other side were more wild blueberry plants. Agatha's heart began to pound. They were close. She could feel it.

But close to what? The real Ax Jack? Was that possible?

"There's a clearing up ahead," Orville said.

Agatha pushed forward eagerly until she stood next to Orville at the edge of the trees. The clearing was more like a giant field in the middle of the dense forest. On one side, a creek cut through the short green grass. On the other side was a shack that appeared to be made of big pieces of corrugated metal haphazardly nailed together.

"This grass has been cut recently," Orville said.

"So somebody lives here." Agatha wrinkled her nose. It was hard to imagine anyone living in that ugly little shack. Who would want to spend their time in such a crazy, drafty place?

A crazy, ax-wielding maniac, she answered herself. Agatha peered at the shack. Sure enough, right in front was a metal rack. It was made of the same kind of metal as the place itself, and it blended with the front wall. But now that she could see the ax stand, it was easy enough to pick out the long wooden handles, the gleaming metal of the sharpened blades. . . .

Agatha tried to swallow down the humungo lump in

her throat. Ax Jack lived here. Who else would have all those axes right outside his front door? The sunlight glinted off the weapons.

Stu was in real trouble! They had to help him right *now*! She ran toward the shack as fast as she could.

"Stuuuuuuu!" she yelled as she bounded over the grass. She wanted him to know that help was on the way. Except . . . wait. If Stu was inside and could hear her, that was okay. But what if Ax Jack were inside? Then he would hear her too.

Maybe running right at the ax murderer's lair and screaming isn't such a good plan, she thought.

Then a sharp pain shot through her ankle. She glanced down quickly—and saw a rope strung between two metal stakes just a few inches above the ground. Her ankle had slammed against it as she ran.

She fell forward . . . and kept falling. The grass below her gave way, tumbling into the hole underneath it. *That was just a layer of sod*, Agatha thought, horrified. *It was camouflage!*

She landed on her face at the bottom of the hole. There was only one explanation: she'd fallen into a trap.

A trap set by Ax Jack.

Orville's pulse increased rapidly when he saw Agatha disappear into a hole in the ground.

He took a deep breath. "Ag—"

Clark slapped his hand over Orville's mouth. His fingers were hot and smelled like onions. And they were touching his face! Touching him! Pressing against him! Blocking out his oxygen!

Orville twisted violently, trying to get away. He hated to be touched. He had to get free! Clark's hand fell away, and Orville took off down the narrow path, putting as much distance as he could between him and the touching.

Clark ran after him.

Agatha fell into a hole, a voice inside Orville's brain reminded him. Slowly his heart rate decreased. He stopped running. Running away from the touching meant running away from Agatha. He couldn't do that, no matter what.

"Sorry. I forgot you don't like to be touched," Clark whispered, skidding to a stop beside him.

"You put your hand over my mouth," Orville said.

"You were about to yell and attract attention," Clark said. "What else was I supposed to do?"

"But Agatha fell in a hole." Orville walked quickly back toward the metal shack. "We have to help her."

"It was a trap," Clark said. "She fell in an Ax Jack trap. If we start yelling for her, he'll hear us. Then he'll get us too!"

Orville reached the open field and stopped. Clark motioned for him to stand behind a tree, so he did. He scanned the field around the shack. There was no sign of Agatha.

But the door of the shack was opening.

Clark sucked in a sharp breath. Orville noticed that his own respiration was shallow. Maybe he was frightened.

An old man appeared at the door. He was tall, with gray hair. He wore denim overalls. And he was picking up an ax from the ax stand. It seemed extremely likely that this was Ax Jack.

Clark moaned a little. Orville wondered if he was frightened too.

Ax Jack started across the field to where Agatha had disappeared. The ax he held had a blade that looked to be about eight inches long and five inches tall, with a handle that came up to his waist. He dragged the ax behind him as he walked.

Orville's heart rate had increased to an astonishing degree. He had never noted it to be so high before. Judging by this, he was terrified. What would Ax Jack do to Agatha?

The old man reached the hole. He stood at the edge, gazing down into his trap.

Is Agatha okay? Orville wondered. *Is she hurt?* There was no way to tell how deep the hole was from this distance. It was possible that the fall had injured her.

Orville watched as Ax Jack raised his weapon into the air.

Chapter 6

Clark whimpered in fear, and Orville's heart gave another lurch as he stared at the ax.

Ax Jack looked up at his ax, turned it around . . . and stuck the handle down into the hole. He held on to the top of the handle just below the blade.

"Go on, missy, grab onto it," his voice floated across the field.

Ax Jack pulled on the huge ax, and Agatha appeared over the lip of the hole, her small hands gripping the wooden handle. Orville's pulse slowed a tiny bit. It was good to see that Agatha was okay.

The old man kept pulling until she was able to get her feet onto solid ground and find her balance. Then he dropped the ax and grabbed Agatha by the back of her jacket. He turned and looked directly at Orville.

"Come on out, young vermin!" Ax Jack bellowed. "I know you're hiding in there!"

"Oh no oh no oh no," Clark whimpered. His breath came in short, fast gasps. Orville recognized the symptoms—Clark was hyperventilating.

Orville stepped out into the field. "Over here," he called.

"What are you doing?" Clark cried.

But Ax Jack was already on his way over, pushing Agatha along by his grip on her jacket. "Let's go, come on," he snapped, gesturing with the ax. "Everybody in front of the house. Line up now."

"Clark is hyperventilating," Orville said. "He is in need of aid."

"That's not my problem," Ax Jack retorted. "Breathing or not, I want you lined up in front of the house."

Agatha shot Orville a meaningful look. He knew it was meaningful, because her eyes were open very wide and her left eyebrow was raised. But he didn't know what it meant.

"You! Short boy!" Ax Jack pointed the ax at Orville. "Stand next to the door."

Orville walked over to the door of the shack and stood still. Agatha and Clark followed him. Agatha was seventy-three percent paler than usual. Clark continued to hyperventilate.

"Turn around and look at me!" Ax Jack yelled. His skin was tanned the color of manganese dioxide flakes. "Look me in the eye, you little trespassing brats!"

Orville looked him in the eye. It was somewhat difficult because Ax Jack's small, pale blue eyes shifted back and forth as he talked. Agatha and Clark were both staring at their feet. Clark was whimpering.

"Now, I'd like an explanation as to what you're doing on my property!" Ax Jack bellowed. He paced in front of them, swinging the long ax forward with every step. The blade dug into the ground with a *thwack* each time he swung. When he yanked it from the earth, dirt flew an average of five inches in all directions. "And after the explanation, you'll be punished! Punished severely."

Suddenly he stopped walking and swung the ax toward Agatha.

Orville heard her quick intake of breath as the blade whipped through the air. Ax Jack was just pointing the blade at her. "You! Talk!" he ordered.

Agatha finally looked up. "Are—are you Ax Jack?" she whispered.

"Yes!" he yelled.

Clark moaned.

"You're real?" Agatha asked, still whispering.

"Do I look like a figment of your imagination?" Ax Jack yelled.

"It would be impossible to look like that," Orville put in. "Because it is impossible to know how figments of someone else's imagination look."

Ax Jack stared at him for 3.1 seconds. Then he turned back to Agatha. "Talk!"

"Please don't hurt us. We're just looking for Stu. And it's totally unfair for you to take him like that, because you're not even supposed to be real. You're like the Trixie of South Haven Park, so nobody thought to be on guard," Agatha babbled. "Not to mention that it's a bad move on your part too because it's been a long time since your last crime and now if you start all over again, the police will find you because there's all sorts of new DNA testing thingamajigs. Tell him, Orville."

"Tell him what?" Orville asked.

"That even if he kills us all, they'll totally find him and nobody's gonna let him make axes in jail," Agatha went on, taking a step toward Ax Jack. "So just give Stu back and we'll forget this ever happened. How's that for a deal?"

Ax Jack stared at Agatha for 3.6 seconds. Then he turned to Clark. "You! You're the oldest. What in tarnation is she talking about?"

Clark opened his mouth, but all that came out was a soft squeaking sound.

"She wants Stu Frysley returned," Orville translated for Agatha. She had a habit of disguising her true intent with extraneous words. Occasionally he had to simplify it for other people.

"Who is Stu Frysley?" Ax Jack asked.

"He's the kid you took," Agatha said. "Remember? You kidnapped him from his tent last night?"

Ax Jack's white eyebrows shot up. "Little lady, pardon my French, but you're a loo-loo! I didn't kidnap *anyone*."

"Oh, please," Agatha said. "You might as well stop lying, because my best friend is a witness. And he gave a full description to the authorities, so even if you get rid of him, they'll still be able to find you. Tell him, Orville."

"Tell him what?" Orville asked again.

"That you saw him in your tent last night!"

Orville looked at Agatha. "But I didn't see him in my tent last night," he said. "I've never seen this man before in my life."

"What are you talking about?" Agatha cried.

"This is not the man I saw in my tent," Orville repeated.

"What?" Agatha was speechless. "I'm speechless," she said. "Seriously, Orville, I don't know what to say. You told us that you saw Ax Jack take Stu!"

"No, I didn't," Orville replied. "I described the person I saw, and many other people decided that it was Ax Jack. You said that Ax Jack didn't exist, so it couldn't be him."

"What's all this about not existing?" roared Ax Jack. "Who told you kids I'm not real?"

Agatha ignored him—and his stupid ax. "But you described him," she said to Orville. "You told us he was an old man with an ax. And this, right here, is an old man with an ax."

"But it's not the same old man," Orville said. "This

man is clean-shaven. The man in the tent had a four-inch-long beard."

"So he shaved," Clark put in. "So what?"

"The man in our tent had extremely large work boots on, which would indicate that he had extremely large feet."

Agatha glanced at Ax Jack's feet. He was wearing flip-flops. Why hadn't she noticed that before? She'd been terrified of a guy with flip-flops? What kind of ax murderer wore flip-flops?

"This man's feet are obviously quite small for his height," Orville went on. "I estimate no larger than a size eight."

"Eight and a half," Ax Jack growled.

"Maybe he wears big shoes when he steals his victims," Clark argued. "You didn't see his actual feet last night, just his boots."

"Yeah," Agatha said. "And you talked about what kind of clothes he was wearing in the tent, but he could have changed since then. Maybe you're getting confused by the different details, like no tan coat and stuff."

"But this man is over six feet tall, and the man in our tent last night was only five-foot seven."

Agatha opened her mouth to explain that away . . . but how? You could shave and change your clothes and your shoes. But how could you suddenly grow five inches or more? "Maybe he was crouching down to grab

Stu, so you misestimated?" she finally said. But she knew that was impossible. Orville would have taken a crouch into account.

"The man in our tent was standing straight up as he pushed Stu through the flap," Orville said calmly. "He was five-foot seven, and he had a large, protruding stomach."

Agatha's eyes went to Ax Jack's stomach. The overalls he wore hung loosely on his thin frame. Really, he was pretty skinny for such a tall guy. She looked way up until she could see his face. He was frowning. "I think I'd better hear this whole story," he grumbled. He grabbed up the ax and sliced it through the air—landing it neatly in the ax stand. "Follow me."

He led them around the shack to a wooden picnic table and four chairs that looked like tree trunks with seats carved out of the tops. "Sit," he commanded.

They sat.

"You brats want lemonade, I suppose."

"You have lemonade?" Agatha asked, shocked.

His brow furrowed as the perma-frown grew even deeper. "Why wouldn't I have lemonade?"

"Well . . . it's weird enough that you have a picnic table. I guess that could be for chopping people up on. But why does an ax murderer need lemonade?"

Ax Jack snorted. "Ax murderer!"

"You said you're Ax Jack," Clark replied.

"The legendary ax murderer," Agatha added.

"No, I said I'm Ax Jack, the legendary lumber artist." The old man ran the back of his hand across his forehead. "The things you kids come up with year after year," he muttered.

"What is a lumber artist?" Orville asked.

"Well, look around, youngster!" Ax Jack cried. "I make things out of unfinished wood. What are you sitting on? Why, that table retails for over a thousand dollars."

Agatha took another look at the wooden table and chairs. They *were* pretty nice.

"And those bears over there go for three, four hundred a pop." Ax Jack pointed to a line of tree trunks standing along the back of the shack. Agatha hadn't noticed them when she sat down, but now she could see that each trunk was carved to look like a grizzly.

"But why do you have all those axes?" she asked.

"It's how I carve," he said. "Folks like a rough-hewn look to their lawn art. Makes 'em feel like mountain men or some nonsense. I'll tell you, it takes a mighty small ax to carve a bear's face. My arthritis acts up something nasty when I use those. I'm thinking the rest of my pieces from now on will be on a grand scale. Only way to avoid those pea-sized axes."

"You're . . . you're just an artist?" Clark asked.

"*Just* an artist!" Ax Jack snorted. "I'd like to see you

make a living through the sheer genius of your creative abilities."

"Your art is made of wood," Orville complimented him.

"It certainly is, mister. Home-grown right here on my own little acre and a half of paradise."

Agatha glanced at the tiny metal shack. "Do you actually sell anything?" she asked doubtfully.

"Sure. My little carved guard dogs sell like hotcakes. Tell your parents—all you have to do is go to axjack.com and order them up."

"Why do you live in a storage shed, then?" Clark asked.

"Because I'm eccentric," Ax Jack said. "And I'm short-tempered. So let's hear the rest of your story before I get ornery."

"We're on a school camping trip and somebody snuck into a tent and grabbed Stu," Clark explained.

"Stu's a friend of yours?" Ax Jack guessed.

"Not even!" Agatha snorted. "Stu doesn't have any friends on account of what a poo head he is."

"Stu is Agatha's number-one enemy," Orville added.

"Well, that explains why you're looking for him," Ax Jack said with a smile. "Why did you think I did it?"

"The person who snatched Stu was dressed like Ax Jack," Agatha told him. "Or, you know, what we thought Ax Jack would dress like. The murderer Ax

Jack. Nobody ever told campfire stories about a lumber artist. Not even my uncle Wilbur, and he tells the worst stories ever. Sorry."

"You say this was last night?" Ax Jack asked.

"It was at four fifty-two this morning," Orville answered.

"I saw them."

"Who?" Agatha asked.

"Your Stu and the other guy," Ax Jack said. "Just after dawn this morning."

Agatha felt like her brain had turned inside out. First it had seemed like Stu had played a prank and pretended he'd been taken by Ax Jack—who didn't actually exist, except in creepy stories. Then Ax Jack had turned out to be real but hadn't snatched Stu. Then Ax Jack had turned out not to be a killer but an artist. And *then* Stu turned up at the real Ax Jack the artist's place anyway. She had a million questions. But all she could think to say was, "Huh?"

"This is my land. I own it," Ax Jack said. "The county's been after me for thirty years to sell them my property. They don't like that I'm smack-dab in the middle of their precious park."

"Okay . . ." Agatha had no idea what this had to do with Stu, but she didn't want to be pushy. There was no point in making Ax Jack more ornery than he already was.

"The dang hikers and bikers and sightseers are

always littering my land, traipsing all over it as if they owned it!" Ax Jack ranted on.

"Yeah, that's . . . annoying," Clark agreed. He shot Agatha a what-is-he-talking-about? look. She shrugged.

"Annoying? It's maddening! It's infuriating! It's illegal." Ax Jack looked at each of them in turn. "When I catch someone in one of *my* tourist traps, I call the police. And I prosecute to the fullest extent of the law!"

"What's the punishment?" Agatha asked.

"A thirty-one-dollar fine," Ax Jack said with a self-satisfied nod.

"What does this have to do with Stu?" Clark demanded. "Because we really have to get back to the campsite, so—"

"Hold your water, Sparky, I'm getting to it." Ax Jack cracked his knuckles. "I'm up before the sun every morning, and I certainly notice people on my property whenever I'm awake. I didn't go after those two. Too bad—apparently it would've saved you a lot of trouble if I had."

"Why didn't you?" Agatha grumbled. It didn't seem quite fair that she'd fallen into a hole and Stu had just gotten to walk right by.

"They were off toward the property line, only stepping onto my land every couple of feet. And they were obviously just passing by, not aiming to pick my blueberries or have a picnic on my front lawn. Why, I've even had people just plop themselves right down where you're sitting without so much as a by-your-leave."

"Are you sure it was Stu you saw?" Agatha asked. "Can you describe him?"

"Well, no. I didn't go after them. It takes my old bones longer to get moving than it used to, and they were gone within a minute or two. But one of them was definitely a kid—I know that for sure. The other one was taller. I didn't notice him looking much like me, though." He gave them the evil eye, as her nana would have called it. But Agatha wasn't even a teeny-tiny bit scared of Ax Jack anymore.

Agatha turned to Clark and Orville. "See, I was right! Stu punked us. Ax Jack saw Stu and his prank partner heading out of the park."

"The two of them didn't look like partners," Ax Jack said. "Didn't look what you'd call friendly to me."

Uh-oh. That didn't sound good. Had Stu actually been snatched by a non–Stu accomplice? "Where did they go?" she asked breathlessly. "We've got to track them."

"No, we've got to get back to camp," Clark said.

"But we're hot on the trail." Agatha decided it was better not to mention the fact that "hot" didn't usually mean "seven hours behind them" when one was on the trail.

"They were over near the creek. That's the boundary

of my land," Ax Jack said. "They walked along on my side for a while; then they crossed the water and headed out of the park."

"How do you know it was out of the park?" Orville asked.

"There's not much park on that side of my property. Just a quarter mile of scrub trees, then the road. If they kept heading in that direction, there's not many places in South Haven they could go."

"That settles it," Clark said. "If they left the park, there's no way we're going to find them. Thank you for your help, sir." He stood up. "Let's get back to camp, you two."

"Hold on there, champ. We haven't talked about your trespassing yet," Ax Jack said gruffly.

Clark froze. "Uh . . . well, we're on a humanitarian mission," he said.

Agatha rolled her eyes. Obviously she was going to have to step up. "Ax Jack, we're sooo sorry we came onto your land without permission. But now that we've seen your truly inspiring work, we can't wait to tell all our friends—"

"And your parents," Ax Jack interrupted.

"Right, and our parents. We'll tell them all about your art and where to buy it."

"That's axjack.com," he said.

"Got it." Agatha began walking as she spoke, Orville

and Clark right behind her. "Thanks again! 'Bye!" She was hoping that Clark would be so distracted by her little conversation with Ax Jack that he wouldn't notice what direction they were heading in.

"We're heading in the wrong direction," Orville said. "The trail is ninety degrees east of here."

D'oh! Why did her best friend have to be so honest all the time? "Um, I kinda want to wash my hands before we start back," she fibbed. "They're covered in dirt from when I fell in Ax Jack's trap."

"I know what you're doing," Clark said. "You're still trying to follow Stu. But it's hopeless. You guys can't solve this case now."

Luckily, he kept following Agatha as he was talking. Only a few more yards and they'd be at the creek.

"Stop!" Orville said. "There are footprints."

Agatha stood still and looked down. The grass had gotten muddy as they walked closer to the creek, and in some spots it had been bent and trampled.

"This is stupid." Clark went right up to the edge of the creek. "What good are footprints going to do now?"

"You're walking on the evidence!" Agatha cried. "Stop right where you are!"

Clark rolled his eyes. But at least he stopped trampling all the footprints. "Orville, go to work," Agatha said.

He blinked at her.

"I mean, tell me what you notice about the foot-prints," she clarified.

Orville stepped carefully around Agatha and went over to the creek. "The clearest prints are in the mud at the water's edge," he reported. "These are the only ones I see that Clark hasn't ruined."

"Sorry. Man," Clark muttered.

"There are at least two different prints," Orville went on.

"Is one of them from Stu?" Agatha asked.

"One is small, approximately a size six. It has treads like a sneaker."

"What size shoe does Stu wear?" she asked Clark.

"How should I know?"

Agatha thought about that. Did she know her cousins' shoe sizes? Well, yes. But only the girl cousins, because she got a lot of hand-me-down shoes. Which was gross. But try convincing Nana of that.

"Stu wears approximately a size six," Orville said. "And he always wears sneakers."

"Looks like we have a winner," Agatha replied. "What about the other print?"

"It's large, consistent with the size of the work boots on the man who took Stu from our tent."

"Size sixteen?"

Orville nodded. "The tread has a brand name

written in it: Hoofers. The footprints lead into the water right here."

"So what?" Clark said. "The old guy already told us all this."

"Let me tell you a basic truth about life that you learn when you're a hard-boiled detective: people lie," Agatha told him. "They lie all the time. Big lies, small lies, omissions of the truth. You'd be surprised."

"Agatha lies an average of three times per hour," Orville chimed in.

"Thanks," she said, frowning at him. "My point is, Ax Jack back there seemed like a nice old man—"

"Not really," Clark said.

"But he could have been a liar. A big, huge, ax-murdering liar," Agatha went on. "We had to check out his story. See if he was on the up-and-up."

"And it looks like he was. Can we go now?" Clark asked.

Agatha stared off across the creek. She really wanted to follow the footprints. But Stu and the Stu-snatcher had been here so long ago. Was there any point in going after them?

"Lunch will start in twenty-one minutes," Orville said. "Ms. Winogrand is sure to notice if we're not there."

"Oh, all right, we can go back," Agatha said. "But this investigation is not over yet. We are going to find Stu, and we're going to find him today!"

Chapter 7

"I can't believe you didn't find Stu," Adam grumbled. "Now that Ms. Winogrand's making us leave early, I'm gonna be home in time to mow the lawn."

Less than an hour later, the whole seventh grade—minus one Frysley—was back on the big purple bus. "Back to Bottomless Lake. Empty-handed," Agatha said to Orville, who sat across the aisle from her again. "Some detectives we are."

Orville didn't answer.

"What did they ask you, anyway?" Agatha hadn't been allowed to accompany Orville to his interview with the park rangers. As soon as Mildred and Clark had told Ms. Winogrand about Stu's disappearance, she'd called in reinforcements. The park rangers had swooped into the campground, taken Orville into the tent with the teachers and Mildred, talked to him for about five minutes, then ordered the rest of the campers to leave.

"They asked me to describe what happened, and I did," Orville told her. "Then Mildred said she thought I was dreaming. She said Clark was telling campfire stories about an old man with an ax, and that's why I thought I saw an old man with an ax."

"And the rangers bought that?" Agatha asked indignantly. It was outrageous. If Orville said he'd seen something, then he'd seen it. End of story.

"They said I probably heard a noise when Stu left—or when he was taken—that woke me up. But they figured the old-man-with-ax part really was a dream. They said I was probably disoriented from waking up suddenly in the middle of the night in a strange place."

"Hmm." Agatha stared out the window. The bus was pulling out of the main drive into the park. Four more county ranger SUVs were pulling in. One of them had a sign that said SEARCH AND RESCUE. A fire truck followed, then an ambulance.

"Why do they need a fire truck?" Rachel asked.

Agatha leaned over to Orville. "This is turning into a big manhunt. I can't believe they're gonna search the park for Stu when we know that he left. Did you tell them that part?"

Orville shook his head. "They didn't ask."

Agatha sighed. The rangers should have been told all about Ax Jack and the footprints. But it wouldn't have occurred to Orville to tell them something they didn't ask about. He had a hard time understanding how things were connected sometimes. And the rangers probably wouldn't have listened anyway.

"We can't give up, Orville," Agatha said. "Sure, everyone else thinks we're off the case, but we know more than the rangers do. We have to keep looking for Stu ourselves. We could be his only hope."

"How are we going to find Stu?" Orville asked.

"Well . . . we should start with what we know. We know that Stu was seen heading out of the park with another person."

"A taller person," Orville corrected her.

"Right. And we know that the taller person wears a size-sixteen work boot."

"A size-sixteen Hoofers-brand work boot," Orville corrected her.

"Right." Agatha thought about that. And, as usual, Orville had hit on the solution to the problem without even realizing it. "Benjamin Orville Wright, you are a crime-solving genius," she said. "It's the Hoofers."

"What is?"

"Hoofers is a shoe brand for big and tall men. My uncle Irv wears Hoofers," Agatha said. "And . . . drum-roll, please . . . Hoofers can only be purchased at one—count 'em, *one*—store in Bottomless Lake."

She waited for the gasp of astonishment from her best friend.

Orville looked back at her until he realized that she was waiting for a reaction. "Oh," he said.

"That's it? That's all you have to say?"

"Yes."

"Orville, it's a lead," Agatha explained. "If we know

where the work boots were bought, we can find out who bought them. And if we find the person who bought them, we find our Stu-snatcher. It couldn't be simpler."

"Good," Orville said. "How are we going to do it?"

"I am uncomfortable." Orville stared around the Big Foot shoe store. They'd rushed over after dropping their packs off at Agatha's house. The place was crowded, and Orville didn't like crowds, but that wasn't his only problem.

"What's giving you the heebie-jeebies?" Agatha asked as they slowly walked down the men's boot aisle.

"I don't like the way it smells in here," he told her.

"Yeah, I'm not a big fan of the new-shoe smell either," Agatha said. "Although it beats new-car smell any day."

"The shoes aren't the problem," Orville said. "It's the feet that smell."

Agatha took a deep breath, then wrinkled her nose. "You're right. And somehow mixing it with foot deodorizer only makes it worse."

"It's an extremely unsanitary establishment," Orville complained. "People put their feet into multiple pairs of shoes. Even if they're wearing socks, the socks can't remain clean throughout the entire process of trying on different shoes."

"Plus not everyone wears socks," Agatha said. "My cousin Eleanor never does. She says nature intended for us to go barefoot. Although I guess that means she wouldn't be trying on shoes. So, you know, never mind."

"Even people who began with clean socks end up with dirty socks," Orville went on. "Which can lead to tinea pedis or other fungal infections."

"Mm-hmm," Agatha said. She led the way to the back wall of the store, where the men's shoes were stacked. "Hoofers, Hoofers, Hoofers," she muttered as she went up on her tiptoes, then crouched down, making sure she didn't miss one boot. "I read on the Net about this guy who treated his foot fungus with his own urine."

"I don't expect that he had much luck with his treatment. The urea in his urine would have softened the skin on his feet and made them even more susceptible to infection," Orville said.

"Gross. And good to know," Agatha told him. "I'm not seeing any Hoofers, are you? Or size-sixteen anythings."

"No," Orville answered. He noticed a box of Peds near the end of the aisle. Peds easily solved the dirty sock problem. A person could use a new pair of the free socks for each pair of shoes he or she tried on. Yet only fifteen percent of the people in the store were using Peds, as far as he could see.

"If you can't buy size-sixteen shoes at a place called Big Foot, where are you supposed to buy them? I mean, do you have to go to a clown-shoe store?" Agatha demanded. "And do clowns even wear work boots?"

Orville took a pair of the Peds. It made him feel more comfortable just to have them with him.

"Hoofers!" Agatha cried.

Orville turned toward her. She was facing a section of bright red boxes with horseshoes drawn on the sides. "Size fourteen, size fourteen, size thirteen, size fourteen, size fifteen, size thirteen." Agatha frowned. "No sixteens."

"Maybe you have to special-order them," Orville suggested. "I have to special-order my shoes."

"That's just because the only shoes you will consent to wear have been discontinued. The shoe store had to contact all the warehouses to track them down for you." She shrugged. "But size sixteen has to be pretty rare. Maybe they wait for somebody to order it instead of keeping it in stock."

"So they *are* special-ordered," Orville said.

"Could be." Agatha glanced around the crowded store. "We need the help of a trained professional." She hopped up on one of the little stools people sit on when they're trying on shoes. She looked around. "You, sir!" she called. "We need help!"

A short man with what Orville estimated to be size-seven feet rushed over. He *tsk*ed at Agatha until she got off the stool. "I want to buy my uncle Irv a pair of work boots. Hoofers are his faves," Agatha said. Her face was redder than usual but by such a small amount that Orville couldn't even estimate a percentage. Still, it was a sure sign she was lying.

Orville focused on letting her lie without correcting or contradicting her. It took every ounce of his will.

"But he wears size sixteen, and I don't see any," Agatha went on. "What do I have to do?"

"You need to place a special order. I can do that for you." The salesman led them toward the bank of cash registers at the front of the store. "Size-sixteen Hoofers, you say?"

Agatha nodded.

"Huh." The salesman grabbed a binder off the shelf under the registers and began flipping through it. "You sure your uncle didn't order them already?"

"Yeah," Agatha said. "Why?"

"Well, I wrote up an order for a pair of size-sixteen Hoofers a couple of weeks ago," the man said. "Don't do many sixteens. I thought it might be the same guy."

"Wow," Agatha said. "Maybe it *was* Uncle Irv. Or somebody else in my family who ordered them for him. What was the name on that order?"

The salesman gazed at her over the top of his binder. Agatha smiled at him, but Orville knew it was one of her three fake smiles. One was for people Agatha thought were stupid. One was for Stu, and it was more of a smirk than a smile. And one was for people Agatha was lying to.

Orville guessed that this was fake smile number three. But he couldn't entirely rule out fake smile number one.

"That's privileged information," the salesman said.

Agatha gasped loudly. And she gave some of the indications that she was about to get louder still. Her fingers twitched, and the tips of her ears turned pink. "Why is that privileged?" she demanded in a voice twelve percent louder than usual. "What's privileged about shoes? People wear them on their feet. Out where everyone can see them."

A baby somewhere in the store started to cry.

"We don't give out information out about our clients," the salesman said firmly.

Agatha smiled, with her lips closed. Not her usual smile. Fake smile number three. "Thank you very much. You've been very helpful."

One hundred percent lie. Orville was certain.

"You smell like new shoes," he complimented the salesman. The man frowned and turned away. That wasn't what Miss Eloise had told him to expect. People were supposed to be flattered by compliments. They were supposed to smile and say thank you. This salesman was clearly rude.

Orville followed Agatha into another aisle. "You were lying," he said.

"Yes. I can't believe it didn't work."

"Not everyone believes you when you lie," Orville pointed out. "Nor should they."

"Yeah, I guess I need to work on my delivery," Agatha said. "But we still need to find out who ordered those Hoofers. Orville, I need you to create a distraction. I'm going to go behind the counter and find the order list." She raced off before he had a chance to say a word.

A distraction. How was he supposed to do that?

Orville found it distracting when people touched him. Extremely distracting.

But he knew that wasn't true for most other people.

He found the idea of people trying on all those shoes with dirty socks distracting. Maybe other people would find it distracting if they knew about tinea pedis.

Orville swallowed hard. Speaking to people he didn't know was difficult. But there were guidelines to help him. *Meet eye, say hi*, he reminded himself. He walked over to the closest customer, a tall man in a cowboy hat. Orville estimated that eighty-eight percent of the men in Arizona owned cowboy hats.

"Hello, sir," he said, forcing himself to look into the man's green eyes. "My name is Benjamin Orville Wright. I was wondering if you have ever heard of tinea pedis."

"Sure have. Athlete's foot. Used to get it all the time in college. Are you selling a remedy?" the man in the cowboy hat asked.

"No." Orville handed over the Peds. "But you might want to use these when you try on shoes."

The man handed the socks back. "I'm fine with what I have on, but thanks."

That hadn't caused a disturbance at all. The man had had fungus growing on his feet, and he still wasn't worried about it.

Orville closed his eyes. He tried to focus. Agatha was depending on him.

Oh. His mother always said it was extremely distracting when his father trained his performing pigs in the house, especially when he did pig calls. The two main calls were the Grunter and the Squealer. The Grunter was the sound a pig made when it was happily eating. That was the call his father used to calm the pigs down.

The Squealer was the sound a pig made when it was in distress. It brought other pigs running to help. That was what his dad used to call the pigs in from a long distance.

Mrs. Wright found that call to be particularly distracting.

Orville tilted his head back and let loose the Squealer.

Ooooo-weeee-weee-wee! Ooooo-weeeeeeee!

The Squealer! Go, Orville, Agatha thought when the little hairs on the back of her neck went back down.

Everyone was staring. The baby strapped in a Snugli on his mom's chest over in the ladies' pumps section began to scream. Mr. Shoes Are Way Too Private to Speak Of rushed toward Orville.

Agatha ran up to the counter. The cashier hadn't moved. She stood watching Orville, her mouth hanging open. "Can you get my friend some water?" Agatha cried. "Or maybe something wooden to bite down on? He might be having a seizure."

The cashier hurried away. Agatha ducked behind the counter, scanning the shelf for the big binder. It wasn't there.

Why wasn't it there?

The Squealer continued. But now Agatha could hear other voices trying to quiet Orville down. She didn't have much time. Where was the book?

Maybe he'd left it on the counter. She had to risk it. She stood up and looked around for the book. No go. But they had a computer! Oh, so nice.

Agatha quickly typed in the word *hoofers*.

A list of all the Hoofers in the store came up on the screen. *Special orders. I need special orders*, Agatha thought. She scrolled down. Yes, here they were. *Hoofers, sneakers, size 15, red. Hoofers, cowboy boots, size 13, tan. Hoofers, work boots, size 16, green.*

Whoop, there it is!

Agatha ran her eyes across the screen to the name of the customer who had placed the order—and it felt like a keg of dynamite had gone off in her head.

Frysley, Clark.

Chapter 8

"That was some mighty fine distractionating you did in there," Agatha told Orville as they walked over to the bike rack. "I got superb information while you were snorting and squealing. Believe it or not, your friend and mine, Clark Frysley, recently purchased a pair of size-sixteen work boots."

Orville blinked. Had Agatha and Clark become friends during the camping trip? "I do not believe I am attached to Clark by affection or esteem," Orville answered.

"Huh? Oh! Okay. Strike the friend part," Agatha said. "What do you think of the clue—Clark and the mighty big boots?" She popped open her bike lock. Ninety-four percent of the time, she didn't spin the dial after she clicked the lock into place. She said it saved time because she didn't have to enter the combination when she came back for her bike. She said no thief would ever try the lock; they just looked to see if there *was* a lock.

Orville dialed in his combination. "Clark couldn't have taken Stu from the tent. Clark was asleep when the Ax Jack impersonator took Stu. I saw him myself."

"I know." Agatha blew up her bangs. Her frustration level was rising at a rate of approximately seventeen percent per hour. "But how weird is it that he bought work boots in exactly the same size as the fake Ax Jack's? Mountains on top of mountains of weirdness is how weird," she continued, answering her own question. "We should tail him."

"Clark was in the tent when Stu was taken," Orville repeated. "And he wears size eight narrow."

"I know. You're right. But my gut is talking. It's telling me that we have to investigate Clark," Agatha said. "The work boots were the only clue we had left. Which makes Clark the only clue we have now. And why is a guy with eight-narrow feet buying size-sixteen boots anyway?" Agatha gave a firm nod. "Yes, this is weirdness that must be investigated."

She straddled her bike. "Okay, Wonder Boy, where are we gonna find Clark?"

Orville pointed at the department store across the street.

"You bedazzle my mind," Agatha told him. She got off her bike and locked it into the rack again—without turning the dial. "How did you do it? Was his tongue stained blue from the Lake Licorice they sell there and you knew he'd be back for more? Those stains *last*. Or, oh, I know!" Agatha gave a little hop. "He had sloppy-joe farts! When I eat Trix-N-Treats sloppy joes, which I have to because they are yummy, they make me fart for a week! Is that it, was he stinkin' up the tent with s.j. farts?"

"His Civic is parked in the parking lot," Orville explained.

"Oh." Agatha paused for approximately nine seconds. "Well, let's get over there."

They crossed the street and walked over to the front doors of Trix-N-Treats. "Surveillance time," Agatha said as the automatic doors wheezed open for them. A familiar mix of smells—the percentages were always slightly different—hit Orville's nose. Lavender floor cleaner and dirty mop water. Fresh popcorn and rancid popcorn oil. Plastic and candy and sawdust in the bottom of the hamster cages.

Orville raised his eyes to the mirrors arrayed at different angles in the ceiling near the cash registers. "Clark is in the soda section," he told Agatha.

Agatha followed his gaze and saw Clark checking out the selection of soft drinks. "Let's go see what our friend—I mean our Clark," she quickly corrected herself, "is doing." She led the way down the aisle next to the one lined with sodas. "I'll just take a peekaboo," she said when they reached the end.

She leaned around the corner of the soda aisle, then jerked back. "Clark just put two six-packs of kiwi soda into his cart. Eww. Nobody drinks kiwi soda."

"I have seen five people drink kiwi soda. That includes the girl with the striped shirt from the kiwi soda commercial," Orville told her.

Agatha did another Clark check. "He's on the move! Toward us! Scramble! Scramble!"

Orville blinked. Scramble? He wasn't sure exactly what—

"Orville, run!"

Agatha dashed down the aisle. She didn't hear Orville behind her. She slammed to a stop and looked over her shoulder. He was running in the opposite direction—toward the approaching Clark. "No!" she called. "Wrong way!"

Orville spun around, accidentally knocking a display of bobble-head unicorns to the floor. He bolted toward Agatha.

"Don't worry about it," Agatha told him when they were safely out of sight in the next aisle. "Those things were way too ugly to live."

"They weren't actually alive," Orville corrected her.

"Thank all that's holy," Agatha said. "Their teeth were as big as Chiclets. That's just wrong."

Orville nodded. But he hated it when he was clumsy.

"Let me check on our acquaintance Clark," Agatha said. Again she did her lean-and-jerk-back maneuver.

Agatha gasped. "He just put a Big Enchilada T-shirt in his cart. No one listens to that band."

"That's not true," Orville informed her. "Gretchen Berg, Stu Frysley, and Chris Pearson each own at least one Big Enchilada CD. And your uncle Boonie owns three."

"Bobble cleanup in aisle four," a bored voice said over the speaker system.

"Hi!" an extremely squeaky voice cried from behind Agatha and Orville.

They turned around. A teenage girl in plaid overalls with her hair in braids stood there smiling at them. Orville estimated that her smile was eleven percent wider than the average person's. "I'm Cindy, and I work in the pet department. I want to tell you about a very special sale we have running—this weekend only. If you buy one hamster, you get to bring home a hamster friend for free!"

"IhaveahamsterHisnameisLeroyBrownHisHabitrail wrapsallaroundmyroomButthankyou," Agatha said without pausing for breath.

Orville was absolutely sure Agatha was lying. He knew she didn't have a hamster. But she was only exhibiting slightly reddened cheeks and minimal voice trembling. Maybe the physical traits varied with the person she was lying to. Or what she was lying about.

Agatha turned around and started to walk away. Orville followed her. Cindy jumped in front of them. "Well, how about getting Leroy a friend?" Cindy asked, planting her hands on her hips. Orville noticed that her nail polish matched the pink part of the plaid in her overalls almost exactly. The bows on the ends of her braids matched the green part of the plaid.

"I'mtheonlyfriendheneeds." Agatha did a fast check of the next aisle over. "He's gone. We need to move!"

Cindy grabbed Agatha by the elbow. "Come on, you're not being fair. Think how many hours Leroy is alone while you're at school."

Agatha didn't usually mind being touched. But she reared away from Cindy—crashing into a six-foot-five-inch-high cardboard display of stuffed puppies whose eyes were extremely out of proportion to their heads.

The puppies fell almost soundlessly to the ground. One bounced off Agatha's shoulder before it landed.

"Don't follow us, Cindy," Agatha ordered as she slowly backed away.

"I was just trying to win a hamster of my own," Cindy whined. "Whoever sells the most gets one."

"Not my problem." Agatha kept backing. "We're here on serious business." Orville wasn't sure why she was walking backward, but in case she had a logical reason, he backed alongside her. Once they were out of Cindy's reach, they turned around and hustled into the next aisle. Agatha did a Clark check. He wasn't there.

"Big-eye cleanup in aisle five," the bored voice called over the speakers.

"Orville. Sneak and creep," Agatha whispered.

"Miss Eloise says those are insulting terms," he replied.

"No! I mean we need to sneak and creep. Like this." Agatha pressed her back against the shelf and inched down the aisle sideways, slowly and carefully. Orville had seen this technique on ninety-seven percent of cop shows he'd seen. But mostly when the cops were carrying guns and they were trying to make sure someone else with a gun wasn't going to shoot them.

That wasn't the situation here.

He followed Agatha in his normal walking mode.

"I don't want a hamster!" a voice cried.

Agatha stopped sneaking and creeping. "That's Clark," Agatha mouthed.

Orville nodded. He recognized the tone and timber of the voice. Although he was surprised at the volume. Clark hadn't raised his voice when he'd heard his cousin was missing. Nor when he'd met Ax Jack.

"What I want," the level of Clark's voice had dropped by thirty percent, "is a DVD or video of *The Happy Family Takes a Vacation*."

"Aisle twelve," Orville heard Cindy snap in response.

"Bad taste must run in the family. Stu is always saying that stupid *Happy Family* line—'I love the stuffing out of this stuff,'" Agatha said once there had been time for Clark to walk away.

"I've heard him say it seventeen times this year,'" Orville agreed.

Agatha pressed both hands to her head. "I'm having a brain explosion."

Orville backed up a step.

"Stu likes *The Happy Family*, right? And Big Enchilada. Is he one of the people who likes kiwi soda?"

"Yes," Orville answered.

"I knew it!" Agatha could hardly stand still. "See, my gut was speaking truth. There *is* something suspicious about Clark. He has to know where Stu is. That's why he's buying all these lame-o Stu-approved items."

Orville could almost feel his mind whirring. "That's not the only possible motive," he said. Figuring out motives wasn't as easy figuring out logical questions. Motives depended very heavily on emotion, and emotion was difficult for him to understand. But he was never going to learn if he didn't keep trying. "Maybe Clark's motive is that he wants to have all Stu's favorite things waiting for him when we find him," he suggested.

Agatha's eyebrows moved together about an eighth of an inch. "Maybe," she said slowly. "That makes sense. Clark must feel really bad about Stu getting snatched right out of the tent that Clark was supervising. Still, I think we should keep following him. He's our only lead," Agatha added. "And my gut doesn't trust him."

"He was heading for aisle twelve," Orville said.

"Right." She gave him a lopsided grin. Agatha had many more real smiles than fake smiles—far too many to catalog.

They rushed toward aisle eleven to get into position for Clark observation. Orville saw a cinnamon drop on the floor, some sawdust, a pair of size-eight-narrow shoes moving toward them, a small—

"Abort, abort!" Agatha shout-whispered. She rushed up the main aisle. Orville followed her to the ice cream freezer. "He almost saw us," Agatha said.

"He did see you." A man stood behind them with his beefy arms crossed over his chest. He was losing his hair in a circle in the middle of his head, and he was wearing a name tag that said HENRY and MANAGER on it. "He saw that the pair of you have required two cleanups in the last ten minutes," Henry the manager added. "And so, because he's a nice man, all he's going to do is ask you to leave. Right now."

Agatha and Orville went quickly and quietly. Agatha led the way over to one of the little plastic tables in front of Trix-N-Treats. She adjusted the cloth umbrella until it blocked most of their view of the parking lot.

"This is still part of Trix-N-Treats," Orville said.

"So?" Agatha rested her head on her arms so she could see under the umbrella. "This is a great spot to see what Clark does next."

"Henry the manager told us to leave Trix-N-Treats," Orville said.

"He won't come out and check," Agatha promised.

Orville felt his pulse accelerate a little. He must be getting nervous. "The sign on the wall also says you're not supposed to be using the tables if you're not eating food," Orville informed Agatha.

Agatha opened her purse, pulled out a box of raisins, and handed them to Orville. He usually didn't eat raisins during the middle of the day, but he wanted to obey the sign. He took five and handed the box back to Agatha. She started to put it back in her purse. "You need to eat some too."

"Oh, right." She dumped some raisins directly into her mouth and continued to watch the parking lot. Orville lowered his head so he could watch the lot too.

"Your pants are crinkly," he muttered as he watched a woman pass by. He figured he could watch for Clark and get some of his social skills homework done. The woman just glanced at him sideways and increased the pace of her walking.

"Her pants are seersucker. Never a good choice, if you ask me," Agatha commented. "Orville, let me make the compliment thing a little easier for you. Just pick what you want to compliment and then add 'looks pretty.'"

"So then I would have said, 'Your pants look pretty,' to that woman?" Orville asked.

"Yes. You would have been lying, but yes," Agatha answered.

"I don't lie."

"Huh. That's true." Agatha bit her lip. "I hate to tell you this, Orville, but that's going to make giving compliments kinda hard. It's all about little white lies."

"But lying is wrong," Orville said.

"Yes. Sort of. Except when it's not." Agatha sighed. "I guess it's just that there are times when it's okay to lie. And there are times when it's not. For instance, it's okay to tell an old lady that she looks pretty even if she doesn't. Because it makes her happy. And it's okay to tell someone that you like their shirt even if you don't. Because you're being nice and giving them a compliment. It's just a white lie."

Orville didn't answer. How was he supposed to be able to tell the difference between times that he could lie and times that he couldn't? That was too confusing. He liked his rules to be black and white: lying is wrong, telling the truth is right. The compliment situation seemed to fall into a gray area. Perhaps Agatha was mistaken. He would have to ask Miss Eloise at social skills class on Thursday.

Agatha leaned so far forward that the yarn fringe on the umbrella gave her a set of orange bangs. "Thar he blows! The Clark!"

Orville leaned farther forward too. "He isn't heading to his own car."

Clark walked over to a 1993 Toyota Corolla with a dent in the left rear side. A long scrape started just after the back door handle and continued down to the dent.

The driver's door opened and a girl stepped out. She was Asian and had short black hair and a tattoo of a butterfly on her shoulder. Clark handed her his two Trix-N-Treats shopping bags.

Agatha made a face that she called cheetah-in-childbirth. "What is he doing? Now he's giving all the Stu stuff to that girl. I don't understand anything anymore!"

Clark put his hands on the girl's face. A shudder went through Orville's body. He was touching her! How could she stand it? Then Clark kissed the girl. Orville couldn't watch.

"Oh, she's his girlfriend!" Agatha exclaimed, completely unconcerned by the touching. "It all comes clear. They're in league. They're a pair. They're a dynamic duo."

"Are they done kissing?" Orville asked as he stared at the fake mosaic on the plastic tabletop.

"Yep. All clear."

He looked up again just in time to see the girl get back in her car and turn up the volume on her radio. She pulled out of the parking spot. People who listened to music while driving got in significantly more accidents. Maybe she didn't know that.

"But why would Clark's girlfriend want all that

stupid stuff from Trix-N-Treats?" Agatha murmured. "I was sure he bought that stuff for Stu."

The girl steered her car past the patio where Orville and Agatha were sitting. She drove with only one hand on the wheel—inadvisable. With her other hand, she tapped along on the side of her car to the music.

"That girl is wearing the ring the Ax Jack in my tent wore!" Orville exclaimed.

"What? What, what, what?" Agatha cried, sitting up fast.

Orville straightened up too. "Blue crystals in the wings, with the club of the left antenna missing," he explained. "I suppose there could be two people with rings like that, but the likelihood of two people in the same area with rings broken on the same antennae—"

"Why didn't you say the faux Ax Jack was wearing a ring?" Agatha interrupted him. "That's a really big clue."

"You didn't ask if he was wearing jewelry," Orville answered. "People asked if he was wearing a tan coat and green boots and if he had an ax. Nobody mentioned jewelry."

"But why would a man with a beard and an ax in size-sixteen hiking boots be wearing a butterfly ring?" Agatha's hands were folded tightly together. Her knuckles were approximately seventy-one percent lighter in color than usual.

Orville blinked twice. "Why wouldn't a man with a

beard and an ax in size-sixteen hiking boots be wearing a butterfly ring?"

Agatha's mouth hung slightly open for a moment. "Because!" she finally burst out.

"Maybe it wasn't a man with a beard and an ax in size-sixteen hiking boots wearing a butterfly ring," Orville said. "Maybe that girl has really big feet—"

"And was wearing a fake beard," Agatha finished for him. "Come on, Orville. We have to find that girl!"

Chapter 9

Agatha's aunt Suzy did not look happy to see her. Agatha ignored the alligator-with-an-ingrown-toenail expression that crossed Aunt Suzy's face the instant she opened the door to them. She also refrained from asking her aunt where she had gotten those hello-I'm-ancient huge pink plastic curlers. "Hi, Auntie Suzy! I need to borrow a book from Serena," she chirped.

Her aunt didn't move out of the doorway so that Agatha and Orville could come in. But behind her, Agatha saw Serena's bedroom door open, and then her cousin popped out like a high-speed jack-in-the-box.

"Agadora!" Serena cried. "Come in, come in. Don't vacillate. I'll get some tea. I'll make a fruit tray. Usurp my bedroom." Serena whipped past her mother and into the kitchen.

"Serena has to study. She is taking the SATs in three weeks." Aunt Suzy lowered her voice to a hiss. "For the second time." Her scowl deepened. As if the alligator now had a second toenail giving her trouble. "You were supposed to be helping her study for the first time. What were you doing all those nights? Reading magazines? Painting your nails?"

"I'm sure Serena will do great on the next test," Agatha said. Even though she wasn't absolutely sure. The first time around, Agatha had learned more SAT vocabulary words than her cousin had. Serena could be a little bit of a fluff head. And she'd just used the word *usurp* wrong. Unless she actually expected Agatha and Orville to take possession of her bedroom by force. "I'll help her study some more," Agatha added.

"No, you won't!" Aunt Suzy snapped.

"Fine. Whatever you say," Agatha answered. "But right now my good friend Orville and I really need that book. And Serena did invite us in for tea and fruit." Aunt Suzy didn't mind being rude to family. But it was harder for her to be rude to people she didn't know that well.

"Not long," she said, pointing at Agatha. Then she smiled at Orville. "Welcome to our house. I've heard a lot about you." She moved aside so they had room to enter.

Orville nodded. "Your curlers are pretty."

Aunt Suzy flushed. She began snatching the curlers out so fast that Agatha was afraid half her aunt's hair was going to come with them. Obviously the rules of the compliment still needed a little refining. But that could come after they found Stu.

Agatha led the way into her cousin's room and shut the door behind them. "I don't know what we're doing here," Orville said.

"Sorry. I would've told you, but I was using all my breath to pedal."

"You did ride your bike approximately eight percent faster than usual," Orville told her.

"Really? That's all?" She'd been pedaling so fast, she'd thought her legs might fall off. "The rangers are looking in the wrong place. And they aren't going to listen to us about where the right place might be. We need to use every second to get Stu back," Agatha told Orville. "Clark goes to high school with Serena. So his girlfriend probably does too. I figure we can find out who she is by going through one of Serena's yearbooks."

There was a bumping sound on Serena's door. Agatha reached over and opened it. Serena came in carrying a tray with cups of tea and a pile of fruit.

"I know it's a rampant collection of fruit, not cut up or anything. But I had to unyoke myself from my mother." Serena set the tray on the bed. "Relish it."

"Uh, nice use on the 'unyoke' and the 'relish,'" Agatha said. "But I'm not sure that 'rampant' is the *r* you were going for."

Serena's face fell. "I hate these asinine words," she complained. She carefully sat down on her bed so she wouldn't spill the tea. Agatha sat down next to her. Orville sat in the chair by Serena's desk.

"I need to look at your yearbook," Agatha told her.

"Which yearling do you want to see?" Serena asked. She handed out the tea.

Bam! Bam! Bam! Serena's door shook as her mother pounded on it. "You said you only wanted to borrow a book. Serena needs to study," Aunt Suzy called from outside the door.

"She's looking for it. My *friend* Orville and I are helping her. Two more minutes," Agatha called back. There was an unconvinced *humph*, then the sound of footsteps walking away. "Um, See-see, a yearling is an animal that's past its first year but isn't two years old yet," Agatha explained gently. "And last year's book would be great."

Serena pulled a yearbook off her bookshelf.

"Do you mind if Orville and I just flip through it?" Agatha asked. "We'll be really careful."

"Sure." Serena handed it over. "Hey, are you guys trying to figure out how to be popular? Because I'm a lot better at that than SAT words. And I would love to help. Love to."

She snatched the book just as Agatha was about to open it.

Agatha wanted to grab it back. But she remembered playing with Serena when they were both little enough to like dolls. Serena would always pack up her Barbies and go home if you didn't do things her way. So Agatha jammed her hands in her pockets and let her cousin flip through the yearbook.

"Look, here's me on the drill team." Serena pointed to a teeny-weeny picture of herself. "I made a lot of friends on that team."

"Cool."

Serena smiled at the picture as if these were people she missed terribly instead of girls she still saw every day.

Turn the page. *Turn the page.* TURN THE PAGE! Agatha thought.

Serena turned a couple of pages. "Ooh! And here's me and John Zimmerman as the cutest couple. You wanna know a secret?"

"Sure," Agatha said. She could tell Orville had already entered the zone. He was gazing at the SHOP AT A MONSTER'S PARADISE promotional calendar on Serena's wall with a blank expression on his face. Orville was forever trying to understand why anyone would shop at Nana Wong's souvenir store.

"Me and John weren't even a couple," Serena admitted. "But we knew we were both really cute, so we decided to pretend to be a couple for a few weeks before the contest." She ran her finger over John's face. "Maybe we *should* be a couple."

Turn the page. *Turn the page.* TURN THE PAGE! Agatha thought.

"Oh, and I love this one. This is me in *Grease*! I was one of the Pink Ladies. It was so fun!" Serena started to hum some song Agatha assumed was from *Grease*.

Turn the page. *Turn the page.* TURN THE—
Wait.

Agatha reached across Serena and snapped her fingers quickly in front of Orville's face. As soon as she could tell he was out of the zone, she pointed to a girl standing on the opposite side of the stage from Serena. "Does she look familiar to you?"

"That's Ax Jack," Orville answered.

"No, it's not. It's Jung Choi," Serena told him.

"So you're friends? Do you know where she lives, by any chance?" Agatha asked.

"No." Serena rolled her eyes. "She played Sandy. She thought she was too good to talk to the chorus. Even though Pink Ladies weren't really chorus. We had names and everything," Serena said. She took a sip of her tea.

"Oh." Agatha sighed. What now?

"Do you have a phone book we can borrow?" Orville asked.

"I can't believe I didn't think of that," Agatha said. "The simplest answer is usually the best answer. A basic detective truth."

"Unless Jung Choi is unlisted," Orville said.

"I doubt that. She'd want her name in print wherever possible. She's an attention hog." Serena reached under her bed. "Viola!" she said as she handed over the book.

"That's a musical instrument. Somewhat larger than a violin," Agatha told her as she flipped to the Cs. "You meant to say 'voila.' It's French."

"No way. I've been taking French for four years." Serena flipped a few more pages in her yearbook. "This is my class picture," she told Orville. "Do you like my hair better the way it is there or the way I have it now? Because I'm thinking of letting it grow out again so I can upbraid it more."

Choi, Choi. Where was the Choi?

There was no Choi?

So much for Serena's attention-hog theory.

"Hello?" Serena said to Orville.

Agatha realized she was a little late coming to his rescue. "He's a boy, See-see. Boy? Opinions on hair? Not gonna happen. Give him a break."

"Upbraid means to reproach," Orville said.

"Reproach, reproach, reproach," Serena said, tapping her head. Agatha didn't think she should be doing anything that might scramble what was inside any more than it already was. Her aunt had clearly pushed Serena over the edge. Her cousin had known a lot more of these words a couple of weeks ago.

"How many hours a day have you been studying?" Agatha asked.

"How many hours a day are there?" Serena asked.

"Twenty-four," Orville answered. Agatha suspected

he was relieved to have an easy pitch after that hair question Serena had thrown at him.

"I think I've been studying more than that," Serena said.

"Okay." Agatha grabbed a *Vogue* from Serena's secret stash and slid it inside the ginormous SAT study guide on her desk. "Spend a little time studying the new eye shadow combos. I'll come over as soon as I can and we'll do flash cards."

Serena gave her a fast hug. "Thanks, Ag."

Bam, bam, bam. "Two minutes are up!" Aunt Suzy yelled from outside the room.

"Do you know anyone who would know where I can find Jung?" Agatha asked.

The doorknob to Serena's room began to turn. In half a minute, Agatha was afraid she and Orville were going to be bounced.

"Cousin Billy," Serena said.

The door opened.

"We're leaving." Agatha jumped to her feet. "Come on, Orville!"

Orville turned back to Serena. "Your hair looks pretty," he complimented her.

Serena's face lit up like a Vegas billboard. "Thank you!" she chirped. "I am totally not gonna grow it out then."

They hurried out of Serena's room, down the hall,

and out the front door. Aunt Suzy shut it so fast behind them that it almost caught the heel of Agatha's sneaker. "Very hospitable," she muttered. "Sorry about that, Orville. But at least we're one step closer to finding Jung. Which means one step closer to finding Stu."

She picked her bike up off the front lawn and climbed on. "Ready to rock and roll?"

"No," Orville answered.

She tried again. "Ready to ride over to my cousin Billy's house and see if he knows where Jung Choi lives?"

"Of course. Let's go."

And they were off. Past the car wash where you drove through Trixie's mouth and let her tongue—well, her multiple tongues—lick your car clean.

Then on past the Sea Monster Museum, which included information on all sea monsters, not just Trixie. Also drawings by John Q. Adams Elementary School kids of Trixie. And, for a reason even Orville couldn't figure out, a display of flying saucers. Was the implication that Trixie had come from another planet? No explanation was given.

When they got to the Trixie fountain—with the floodlights that turned the water pink at night—they made a left, a quick right, then Cousin Billy's house was the second one down. He was outside playing basketball with two of his buds.

"Hey, Agatha. You were on that trip with that kid who got lost, huh?" Billy asked, bouncing the ball from hand to hand.

"Yeah," Agatha said. "Orville was right in the same tent."

She could tell the guys thought that was cool. Guys. They sometimes befuddled her the way the world befuddled Orville.

"I was just over at Serena's and she thought you might know where Jung Choi lives," she told her cousin.

Billy dropped the basketball. He turned and walked into his house without a word.

"Ooh," the buds said in a chorus once the door was shut behind him.

"What was that?" Agatha asked, staring at the closed door.

"You said the *J* word," the shorter of the two buds answered.

"You gotta give me more than that." The guys looked at each other. "Come on, one of you talk. It's okay. We're related. And eventually any kind of secret information gets around the family. Am I right, Orville?" Agatha asked.

"It cannot be determined, because the information is secret. There is no way of assessing how much secret information has not been disclosed," Orville said.

It was hard for Agatha to determine when Orville would be good backup and when he wouldn't. He was completely honest, so she'd thought he'd just say that everyone in Agatha's family blabbed about everything. But apparently she'd thought wrong.

"Look, your cousin got his heart broken by Jung, that's the deal," Short Bud said.

"He can't even hear her name without freaking. So don't go asking about her," Tall Bud added.

"Was he going out with her or something?" Agatha couldn't believe a nugget that tasty hadn't gotten passed around the family.

The buds looked at each other again. "Not exactly," Tall Bud said.

"But that doesn't mean he's not hurting. Especially since she's going out with the biggest loser in the school," Short Bud added.

"Clark Frysley," Agatha supplied.

The buds nodded in unison.

"I think my cuz needs a woman to talk to," Agatha said. "Orville, will you wait for me? I think Billy will feel more comfortable one-on-one."

"Okay," Orville said.

"Don't tell him we told you anything," Tall Bud called after her as she crossed the lawn.

Agatha gave him the wave without turning around. Which could mean yes. Or could mean no. She headed into the house without knocking. That was just how it was done at the Brown family house. "Hello, my bubelehs," Agatha called.

"I want to be alone," Billy answered from behind his bedroom door. No one else replied, which was pretty normal. Billy's sister competed in dance competitions, and his brother was always on whatever sports team was going. So there were lots of practices, games, and performances—all requiring parental chauffeuring.

Agatha walked upstairs and into Billy's bedroom. She figured knocking was pointless. He wasn't in the mood to invite her in. There would be no fruit trays—rampant or otherwise—or tea from Billy. He probably wouldn't even give her a piece of that sour apple gum he was chomping.

"I'm very good at listening," Agatha said as she sat down on the bed next to her cousin. The comforter was a mass of lumps under his legs. When was the last time he'd made his bed—elementary school? If he wasn't careful, he was going to grow up to be as big a slob as Uncle Boonie.

"I don't have anything to talk about," Billy said. He stuck another piece of gum in his mouth, and no sirree bob, he did not offer her even half a piece. The stench of sham green apple filled the room. Smelling it while chewing it was one thing. Somehow non-vomitous. It was completely different when it was only in someone else's mouth.

"Look, Billy, I know how it feels to have your heart broken," she told him. Actually she didn't. But she did know how it felt to have Jack Simmons, her absolute *crunch*, call her Abigail. Abigail. And that was something. Her heart had at least been chipped by that little incident.

Billy almost spit out his gum. "What is that supposed to mean?"

"Just that I know how you feel about Ju—" Billy's muscles tensed. Like he was getting ready to bolt again. "That I know how you feel. And I thought maybe that you might want someone—a girl—to sort of talk to, um, some other girl, and see what the first girl could find out from the second girl about how the second girl feels about, uh, guys at her high school."

"Huh." Billy blew a big green bubble. Agatha badly wanted to pop it. Because big bubbles were really fun to pop. But that would cause a delay. It might even cause Billy to order her out of his room. And the Stu clock was ticking. So she resisted the temptation.

Billy sucked the bubble back into his maw. "You think this girl might tell this other girl why she talked to this guy this one time at the drinking fountain and never again?"

That was the cause of the heartbreak? Billy was teetering on the pathetic precipice. But Agatha didn't let on.

"Girls, we like to talk. About almost everything," she

said. "But a conversation like that, it should happen in person. Do you know where a girl who might like to talk to me lives?"

"Twenty-three thirty-two Bluebell Lane." Billy jumped up and pulled Agatha off the bed. "Do you need water for the bike ride over? Gatorade? PowerBar?"

"I need to give you a lying alert here," Agatha told Orville.

"I've been making observations so I will be able to tell when you are lying without you telling me," Orville informed her.

"Great." Agatha smiled at him. "That will be really useful. Here's my plan. We'll tell whoever opens the door that we're starting a housecleaning business and we'll offer them an insanely low rate. But we need to see the inside of the house. . . ."

Her words trailed off and she let out a sigh of the doomed. "If Jung opens the door, that won't work. She'd never let us inside. And she'd also realize that we are on to her and Clark. They'd move Stu the second we got out of smelling range—and that's very fast, because we're both very clean people."

"I don't think anyone is home," Orville answered.

"Okay, hit me," Agatha said.

"The number-one rule in social skills class is never to hit any—"

"Sorry. Allow me to translate the Agatha. I just meant tell me how you know."

"The lights in the kitchen, the back room on our side, and the floodlights in the backyard all went on at precisely the same second. Statistically, that occurs much more often when a timer system is used than when three people are acting together," Orville explained. "Also, that small white dog whose nose is protruding from the back gate has now been barking for approximately two minutes and thirty seconds with neither the owner yelling at it to stop nor one of the neighbors yelling at the owner to tell the dog to stop."

"Works for me. Let's see if we can find any signs of Stu." They leaned their bikes against the hedge of the house they'd been snooping from and scurried up to Jung's house. The yapping of the white dog—its fur was so long, it didn't look like it had feet—went apoplectic.

"Just some kids starting a cleaning business," Agatha told it as they went by. Why waste a good lie? But it was wasted anyway. The dog kept barking as if it had consumed triple its weight in caffeine.

Agatha paused by an artistic grouping of three large cacti in some colored gravel. "Just in case there are three people in there with amazing timing, let me do a quick ding-dong ditch. You stay here with the pricklies," she told Orville. "I'll be right back."

Agatha dashed up the two steps to the front porch, zapped the doorbell, then vaulted over the porch railing and darted back to Orville. She gazed at the door through the arms of the closest cactus as she muttered, "One bananarama, two bananarama, three bananarama."

"A watch is easier. It's now been two-point-five seconds. Two-point-seven seconds."

"I don't know how many point seconds it takes someone to open a door," Agatha told him. "But I know it usually takes between one and seven bananaramas."

"I estimate that house at twenty-one-hundred square feet," Orville began. "The average older person walks four-point-nine-five feet per second. So the longest time, using that average—"

"No offense, Orville, but the bananaramas have pretty much always worked for me, except that one grievous time at Halloween that you and I have agreed never to talk about," Agatha said. "I think we're safe. Let's do a window check."

Agatha headed for the closest window. The curtains were closed. Curtains were *not* a detective's best friend.

She moved down a window. This one had no curtains in the way. It was clearly the bedroom of somebody who watched way too many home-decorating shows. The bed had a mosquito-netting canopy. Stenciled mangoes and oranges traveled around the top of the wall. One wall was painted lemon yellow. There was a lime tree in a brass pot in one corner. The bedspread was watermelon pink, with pillows in every other shade of fruit you've ever seen. The carpet was a normal sandy color. But there were cherry throw rugs—with stems—every few feet.

Lots of bad taste, Agatha thought. Just a whole different brand of bad taste than Stu's. There wasn't a Big Enchilada T-shirt or a kiwi soda can in sight. Although the owner of the room might also enjoy kiwi soda, she supposed.

Agatha hurried back over to Orville. "Anything?" Wait, that was a dangerous question with her friend. "Anything that made you think Stu had been in the house?" she quickly clarified. One thing about being best friends with Orville—it forced her to choose her words more carefully than she would have otherwise. She imagined that would come in handy when it was her turn to take the SATs.

"No," Orville said.

"Let's see the sights in the backyard, shall we?" Agatha suggested.

"The dog is back there. And it's still barking."

"You and I have faced down wolves, Orville Wright. We're not going to let a mini-Muppet stop us, are we?" Agatha asked. Then she realized he hadn't been looking for a pep talk. He'd just been stating information.

Agatha rushed over to the back gate. She lifted the latch and opened the gate slowly. She used her leg to block the munchkin Muppet from making a getaway. It latched its tiny white teeth into the hem of her jeans, and for the first time, the dog's barking stopped.

Agatha hopped into the backyard, the dog hanging from her uplifted leg. She leaned on the side of the house and used both hands to pry the little thing's teeth off her. It must have had teeny-weeny little brain if Orville was right about the big brain/weak jaw correlation, because it had Agatha's pant leg in a death grip.

The second the dog's mouth was available for use again, it started to bark. Agatha slid down the side of the house to stay out of view. She saw something up in the branches of the elm tree near the center of the yard—and froze.

Because in the tree was a tree house. Could there be a better place to hide someone?

Her gut started talking to her big time. Make that shrieking.

Stu's in that tree house! Stu's in that tree house! Stu's in that tree house!

Agatha turned to Orville and put her finger to her lips. Then she pointed to the tree house. "I think that's Stu's prison," she whispered. "Let's go get him out of there."

They ran across the lawn. They would be easy to spot if someone looked out the tree house windows. The floodlights were bright, and the sky was just turning from blue to gray. But no one shouted out an alarm before Agatha began to climb the ladder.

"The third step is a little wobbly," she told Orville under her breath. "Be careful."

He nodded. He looked pale to Agatha, but she didn't bring it up. She thought it might cause him more freakage. Just because he'd climbed through a window yesterday didn't mean he was comfortable with this sort of physical activity.

Agatha reached the trapdoor that led to the tree house. She didn't know if Clark and Jung were up there with Stu. She didn't know if they had Stu tied up or what.

Only one way to find out, she thought.

Wham! She used both hands to slam the trapdoor open.

Stu was lounging on a double-wide orange beanbag. His eyes went wide when he saw her. "Wong, you made me spill my soda!" He held up a can of Kiwi Kapow. "And it was almost full."

Agatha climbed into the tree house. "Stu, Orville and I are here to rescue you," she announced as Orville climbed into the house behind her. "Let's go!"

Stu shifted around until he found a more comfy position in the chair. "No way! I'm not going any-where." He gave a loud burp and nodded at Orville. "Now get me another soda, would you, retardo?"

Chapter 10

"No, he will not get you a soda!" Agatha snapped. She had the urge to punch. But Orville's social skills teacher was right. Hitting shouldn't ever be an option. At least not when you were in middle school and trying to actually be a civilized and mature member of society.

"Then get out of here. Both of you." Stu stood up and grabbed himself a Kiwi Kapow from a cooler stuffed with them. He popped the top, drained half the can, and gave a burp that lasted at least two bananaramas. Extreme nasty.

"Stu, what are you talking about?" Agatha demanded. "We may only have minutes to get you to freedom safely."

"Maybe you're the true retardo." Stu laughed. "I don't wanna leave. I have a sweet deal going. And you two are not going to blow it for me. Vamoose! Be like a cereal and say Cheerio."

"What are you, in first grade?" Agatha cried. "I. Am. Not. Leaving. This. Place. Without. You." She knew she sounded like the noxious Ms. Winogrand, but she didn't care.

Stu grabbed another soda out of the cooler. He

shook it up and down as he yelled, "We'll see about that."

"Oh, no, you will not," Agatha shrieked.

Orville put his hands over his ears.

Agatha grabbed two cans of soda and started to shake them. Stu popped the tab on his can. Kiwi Kapow exploded all over Agatha's face and her Mr. Clean T-shirt.

She retaliated with a one-two pop-pop, hitting Stu with two jets. His hair got plastered to his head and his T-shirt got soaked too. "Hey, this is new!" Stu shouted as he ran his hands over the Big Enchilada tee.

"Hey, that is lame. No one listens to that band," Agatha shouted back.

"That's not true," Orville informed her, hands still over his ears. "Gretchen Berg, Stu Frysley, and Chris Pearson each own at least one Big Enchilada CD. And your uncle Boonie—"

"Nobody with even the tiniest sheen of coolness," Agatha told Stu.

"I agree," said a new voice. An unfamiliar voice.

Agatha jerked her head toward the sound. And saw Jung Choi. Standing between them and the trapdoor. *Uh-oh*, Agatha thought. She hadn't even heard their perp climb in. She'd been too busy fighting with Stu.

I should have had Orville wait at the bottom of the tree as a lookout, Agatha thought. *Now I'm trapped up here with one of Stu's kidnappers.*

Yikes. Make that both of Stu's kidnappers. Clark's blond head appeared through the trapdoor.

There was no escape.

Orville cautiously uncovered his ears. The volume of speech had gone down since Agatha and Stu had stopped spraying soda at each other.

"We don't want any trouble from you two," Agatha told Clark and Jung. "We found Stu, and we're taking him home."

The tree house was too small for five people. Orville positioned his hands in front of his body and placed one of his legs in front of the other, putting most of his weight on one foot. But he was still in danger of people touching him.

The air felt hot. Orville's face felt hot. Approximately eight percent hotter than it had when he'd been on the ground. Approximately thirty-two percent hotter than it had before Clark and Jung had entered the tree house.

"How did you find us?" Clark asked. "I told you to stop looking for Stu when we were back at the park!"

"You just never listened," Agatha said. "I told you we were good! We're detectives. We don't stop until we've solved the case."

Orville's eyes darted around the tree house. It seemed unlikely that whoever had constructed it had made their calculations based on occupation by five people—especially five people of their size. Clark and Jung especially were large. The height of the roof led him to believe it had been built for shorter, smaller people.

His fingers started to tingle. Conversely, his toes began to go numb.

"But I told you to stop!" Clark argued. "You're supposed to listen to me! I was your counselor." He turned to Orville. "You follow rules. Why didn't you stop looking when I said to?"

Orville didn't answer. Clark was not his top priority at the moment. He had noticed another problem with the planning of the tree house. It had been built mainly across two long branches. Long branches caught the wind easily and tended to twist. And the entire tree house was basically a wind catcher itself. The leverage of the force of the wind on the house would be less if the house were in the lower third of the tree. But this house was in the upper third by what Orville estimated was 0.91 meter.

Orville hadn't been able to check the wind speed on his anemometer this morning the way he usually did. His mother hadn't allowed him to bring the device on the camping trip because it had been a present from his grandma Hafner.

"Is he okay?" Jung reached for Orville.

He stepped back, trying to escape. Someone, Orville

wasn't sure who, his vision blurring, bumped into him from behind. A shriek erupted from his throat. He had to get out of here. The only way the tree could react to too much wind speed was to lose part of its structure— leaves, small branches, large branches. That would relieve the pressure. But it could bring down the tree house.

And even if the wind speed wasn't that high today, there were too many people inside. Many too many people.

He hurled himself at the trapdoor and scrambled down the ladder. Agatha's voice spoke inside his head, reminding him of the wobbly step, and he reached the ground safely.

Followed almost immediately by Agatha, Jung, and Clark.

Had they come to the same conclusion about the tree house's lack of safety?

"Don't stand too close to him," Agatha said.

Orville realized his breaths were coming in harsh pants. He did what Miss Eloise had taught him and focused on breathing. Nothing else. In through the nose. Out through the mouth. Nice and slow.

"You're feeling better," Agatha told him.

Orville realized that his pulse was almost normal, and his breathing had calmed down. Agatha had known his symptoms were reduced before he had. "Yes."

"Then it's time to deal with the dynamic duo." She looked back and forth between Jung and Clark. "You two are kidnappers. You've been holding Stu hostage. You are in huge trouble."

"I guess we *are* kidnappers—technically," Jung said. "But Stu's the one holding me and Clark hostage. He's making us buy him things and bring him his food and wait on him like we're his servants."

Jung sniffled. Orville thought about the social skills work sheet he carried around with him to help him identify emotions. There was one picture where a girl was holding a tissue over her nose and tears were running down her face and her mouth was turned down. He checked Jung's eyes. They were approximately sixty percent wetter than the average person's. As he watched, one tear slid over her bottom lashes. He checked her mouth. Turned down. She was sad.

"We didn't plan to kidnap him. It's just that Stu is such a little brat," she finally burst out.

"I hear that," Agatha said.

"I hear that too," Orville agreed. It was very easy to hear Jung. She was standing quite close. A little too close. Orville took one step back. He'd still easily be able to hear Jung.

"It wasn't Jung's idea," Clark said quickly. "The whole thing started because Stu is always trying to humiliate me and I just wanted a chance to get back at him, okay?"

Orville decided to try to analyze Clark's emotional state. Eyebrows pulled together. Corners of the mouth pulled down. Eyes narrowed. Orville thought Clark fit into the angry category.

"So you did all this to teach Stu a lesson?" Agatha asked.

"Well, he also stole my green bunny eraser and I wanted it back," Clark explained.

"Your what?" Agatha said.

"I know it sounds stupid. It's just an eraser. But I've had it since the third grade, when I won it in a spelling contest. And I love it." Clark's eyes widened and his cheeks reddened. "Stu doesn't care about it. He only took it because he knows . . . He knows it's important to me. Ever since he stole it, he never lets it out of his sight."

Jung gave his shoulder a rub. "We figured if Ax Jack asked for the eraser back . . ."

"Stu would cough it up," Agatha finished for her.

"So I told all those scary Ax Jack stories," Clark said. "Stu's always calling me a chicken. I figured it would be cool to make *him* scared for a change."

"I dressed up like Ax Jack—the beard, a mask, those gigantic boots. I had to stuff them. Plus the rest of me," Jung added. She wiped the tears off her face with the backs of both hands. "I was only going to keep Stu out of the tent for about ten minutes, just long enough to scare him into giving me the bunny eraser. Then I was going to let him go."

"It was going to be so perfect. Stu would have run back into the tent, saying Ax Jack had snatched him. Everyone would have laughed and laughed." Clark closed his eyes for a long moment, then opened them and continued. "They would have called *him* a chicken. He would have looked like a scared little kid. Total humiliation. And I would have had Mr. Bunny back."

"It would have been crazy awesome," Agatha agreed.

"But everything went wrong, because Orville was awake." Clark shook his head. "He saw Jung grab Stu. And that's when the whole plan was ruined."

Jung glanced up at the tree house. "I don't like talking about our massive failure where you-know-who can hear us," she whispered. "Let's go in the house."

Agatha did a quick check of the decor inside Jung's house. She had to admit that she kind of liked the girl. Who wouldn't want to put a little scare into Stu? And it was cool that Jung didn't want Stu to have a gloat fest, sitting up there in his beanbag chair, burping away.

But the ugly fruit-based decorating might have been Jung's. And if so, it was unforgivable. Still, as far as Agatha could see, the foolish fruit-loving decorator hadn't made it out of the bedroom. Maybe Jung's parents were the ones with bad taste.

She was surprised she could see that. She was surprised she could see anything. She'd thought the smoke that she was sure was still coming out of her ears would have blinded her. Stu was such a selfish, spoiled, horrible little thing that he should have lived under a rock. Except that wouldn't be fair to the earwigs and slugs and other things that lived under rocks.

"Let's go in the kitchen," Jung said. "I just made brownies with sour gummy worms, M&M's, and of course more Cheez Doodles for Prince Stu. But I made some with just the M&M's, too."

Even the thought of extra-chocolate brownies didn't cool Agatha's mad fever. But that didn't stop her from taking one after they were all seated around the kitchen table.

"Anything to drink?" Jung asked.

"Anything but Kiwi Kapow." Agatha felt her hair. She had half of a hard, sticky helmet up there from the drying kiwi grossness.

"I refuse to have that stuff in our fridge," Jung answered. "So . . . grape, cherry, cola, cherry cola . . ."

Jung's list got longer and longer. She offered milk shakes, smoothies, even soup. She really, really doesn't want to talk about this, Agatha realized. She stood up and grabbed the first can of soda her hand came in contact with. "Orville would like a glass of water. And then we want to know everything that happened. Please." She sat back down.

Clark poured a glass of water and put it in front of Orville. Then he and Jung sat at the table and pulled their chairs very close together. Agatha noticed that Jung had dark circles under her eyes. And Clark had a tiny twitch in his eyelid. Stu had clearly been driving them slowly nuts. Well, not so slowly.

"As soon as I heard you guys looking for Stu, I pulled off my mask and told him the whole thing was a joke," Jung began. "I was sure that he would run right back to the campsite and tattle to the teachers on me and Clark. Then we'd get punished. But it was the only thing to do. I couldn't just keep him and let everyone think he was missing. . . ."

Jung and Clark looked at each other. She nervously twisted her butterfly ring around her finger. "But my little cousin Stu had other ideas." Clark picked up where Jung left off. "He said he wasn't going back. He said that Jung had to take him back here—after he got some of his disgusting trail mix for the road. I had to hand it off to Jung in the Quick-E-Mart parking lot. As if he couldn't survive the fifteen minutes it would take to get home without it."

"He just wanted to torture us," Jung muttered.

"That's why you didn't know the proportions. It wasn't your trail mix," Orville observed.

"Right." Clark twisted his head back and forth, and Agatha could hear his neck popping. "Jung set him up in the tree house while we were supposedly searching for him." He suddenly got very interested in a tiny crumb on the table. "Sorry about that."

Agatha hadn't thought about that part. Clark had let them go tromping around the woods, facing down wolves and an old man who'd called them brats. Clark had let them think that Stu might end up dead!

Of course, now Agatha kind of wished he had.

"You should have told us the truth, Clark," Agatha burst out. She suddenly remembered Orville dive bombing down from Willa Myer's window. "Orville could have really hurt himself at that ranger's cabin. Or—"

"We *are* really sorry," Jung jumped in. "It's just that Clark told us he would report us to the rangers for kidnapping him if we told anyone."

"Or if we didn't give him everything he wanted," Clark added.

"We didn't know what the rangers would do to us." Jung grabbed Clark's hand and held on tight.

"Kidnapping is a felony," Orville said.

"I know. Which means jail," Jung continued. "And now with the manhunt going on . . . everything just keeps getting more out of control. All those people looking for Stu. Helicopters, dogs. It just gets worse and worse every minute."

"My parents called Stu's parents, and they're coming

home from their vacation early," Clark said miserably. "My aunt is losing it, she's so worried."

"Does Stu know about the manhunt?" Agatha asked.

"Of course. He has a TV and a DVD player up there," Clark said. "Jung had to convince her parents that she gets more studying done in the tree house—because it's so peaceful—and that she needed to run an extension cord out there to get light."

"I don't know what we're going to do. I just don't," Jung burst out.

Agatha stood up. "I'll be back in a few minutes."

"Where are you going?" Clark asked.

"I'm going to fix your little Stu problem," Agatha told him. "It will be my extreme pleasure."

Chapter 11

I have so got you, Stu Frysley, Agatha thought as she marched out to the tree house. *You don't know it, but you are chipped beef on toast, my friend.* Orville's face flashed into her brain. *Okay, scratch the friend part. You are chipped beef on toast, my enemy.*

She climbed the ladder. "Got you, Stu," she whispered to herself over and over, one word per step, until she got to the top.

"Get lost, A-gag-atha," Stu said the second she stuck her head through the door.

Agatha ignored him and climbed up into the tree house and sat down across from Stu. She simply watched him. She had him where she wanted him. Actually, so did Clark and Jung—they just hadn't realized it.

"I guess my cousin and his babe have told you the deal by now." Stu crossed his hands behind his head and leaned back in the beanbag chair. "Am I brilliant or what? I had to come up with my plan this fast." He snapped his fingers. "And I did. The second Jung whipped off the old-man mask. Yeah. Brilliant. That's me."

"What you are is in trouble," Agatha informed him. "Huge, huge, gigantic, world-shaking trouble."

Stu grinned. "I think you've got me confused with Clark and Jung."

Agatha leaned forward. "Let me spell it out for you, Mr. Brilliance. There is a manhunt going on for you. Rangers are searching South Haven County Park for you inch by inch. Helicopters are involved. Dogs. The police."

"I know. Which is why Clark and Jung are in so much trouble. They kidnapped me. They started the manhunt," Stu explained, talking slowly and extra-clearly, like he was a deranged kindergarten teacher.

Agatha answered him, speaking even more slowly and even more clearly, like a deranged kindergarten teacher who had been shipped off to a nice quiet place for a nice long rest. "Stu, sweetie, you knew about the manhunt and you didn't come out of your fantasy tree house. You sat up here swilling soda and watching the worst movie ever made."

Stu's eyes widened. Agatha thought she might be starting to get through to that big tater he used for a head. "You're sitting on your lazy butt, having a one-boy party—your usual kind—while the entire world is look-ing for you. They're spending oodles and oodles of money on the search for you. Your parents are freaking out. They think you're lost in the woods. You are letting them believe that you're in danger. When they find out that you've been sitting up here, knowing all this, they're going to punish you forever."

"What am I gonna do?" Stu jumped to his feet. "Agatha, you have to help me!"

"Don't you mean, 'A-gag-atha, you have to help me'?" she asked.

"What? I don't know what you're talking about. So what should I do? Should we go get Orville?"

"You mean retardo?" Agatha asked.

"That's just a pet name. Like buddy," Stu protested. "Should we get him? Maybe he could help us."

"We don't need to waste Orville's time," Agatha said. "I know exactly what you have to do."

"What?" Stu cried.

"Fetch me a can of that kiwi soda." The drink was the last thing she wanted. But she really, really wanted to make Stu play fetch after all he had put her through.

Stu dove to the cooler on his belly, grabbed a can of soda, then returned to Agatha and gently placed it in her hand. "I'm not thirsty after all," she told him. She made Stu wait a nice, long ten bananaramas. Then she told him her plan.

"All you have to do is come forward and tell everyone you've been in Bottomless Lake the whole time. You can say you were scared to be in the woods at night. You couldn't sleep. And you were feeling homesick. So you snuck out of your sleeping bag and snuck home. Your parents are on vacation. And your brothers are staying with Clark's parents—so it makes sense nobody saw you."

"But Orville told people he saw someone take me!" Stu protested. "I heard it on the radio."

"Then you also must have heard that the rangers thought Orville was dreaming when he saw a man take you from the tent. They thought he probably saw something but that he filled in the details from those Ax Jack stories Clark told," Agatha said. "They'd probably believe that Orville just saw you leaving the tent on your own."

"But I'll look like a big baby," Stu whined.

Agatha smiled. "Yes, you will. But would you rather look like a big baby—or be sent off to reform school?"

Orville didn't think there was a face on his work sheet that matched Stu's. His face was red, indicating embarrassment. But tear-streaked, indicating sadness. The position of his mouth fell into the anger category. His eyebrows were raised, which pointed to surprise. And he didn't meet anybody's eyes as he stood in front of Orville, Agatha, Clark, and Jung in the kitchen.

"Okay, Stu. You can use this as a rehearsal." Agatha pointed to Jung, Clark, and Orville. "They are the very nice, very heroic park rangers who have been looking for you."

Stu's face grew redder.

"Start talking," Agatha ordered. She sat down next to Orville. "And be polite."

"Hello. My name is Stuart Frysley. I am the boy you have been looking for. I'm sorry that you all wasted your time and effort. But you see, I got very frightened after my cousin Clark told scary stories about Ax Jack."

"Cut!" Agatha interrupted. "There's no need to name names. Someone was telling scary stories." She clapped. "And action!"

Stu pulled in a deep breath. "I got very frightened after *someone* was telling scary stories around the campfire. I couldn't sleep. I kept thinking about my house and my room. . . ."

Orville noticed that Agatha was mouthing the words along with Stu.

"And my own safe little bed." Agatha smiled as she soundlessly said those words.

"I know I should have told someone," Stu continued, looking at the ceiling. "But I just wanted to be home."

"Eye contact!" Agatha barked.

"My parents are out of town, and my brothers are staying with my aunt and uncle," Stu said, moving his eyes from Clark to Jung. "I could have gone there. But it wouldn't have been the same." Stu sucked in another breath. "I didn't know that there was a manhunt going on for me. I didn't watch TV or anything. I mostly stayed under the covers with my teddy bear." His mouth twisted into a grimace.

"You need to work on the emotion in that last part. I just didn't believe you. I didn't feel it here." Agatha put both hands to her heart. Then she turned to Orville, Jung, and Clark. "So what do you think, guys? Problem solved, no?"

Clark kept opening and closing his mouth—but no sound came out.

'Wow," Jung said. "Just . . . wow. You're brilliant. This is a brilliant plan."

Orville felt the pH level change in his stomach, dropping as the gastric acid became more acidic.

"Oh, and one more thing. Stu . . ." Agatha tapped the table in front of Clark.

Stu dug in his pocket and pulled out a green rabbit-shaped eraser. He held it with two fingers, as if it were radioactive, and set it down before Clark.

"How did you do that?" Clark asked, his voice so soft, Orville had difficulty hearing it. "You were only in the tree house for, like, five minutes and you got Mr. B. back." He picked up the eraser and cradled it loosely in his palm. "I came up with the whole kidnapping plan and I still couldn't make Stu—"

Yes, the contents of Orville's stomach were definitely becoming more acidic.

"'Cause you're a wimp, and you'll always be a wimp, Linguini," Stu told him.

"Stu!" Agatha cried. "Have you already forgotten that we hold all the cards here? You—swilling soda and eating trail mix. Rangers—tromping through the park, searching for a boy in danger. And us—braving the real live Ax Jack to save you."

Stu's face paled by five percent. He held up his hands in surrender.

"I feel so stupid," Jung exploded. "I didn't even think of this. Of course Stu's in huge trouble."

Agatha winked at her. "You had the magic all along, my dear. All you had to do was click your heels together three times and say, 'There's no place like home.'"

"I don't understand," Orville said. The acid level in his stomach was up another two percent. He could feel it burning his stomach lining.

"It's from *The Wizard of Oz*," Agatha explained. "I just meant Clark and Jung had what they needed to make Stu turn himself in all the time. They just didn't realize it."

Orville shook his head. "Not that. The plan. Is the plan to have Stu lie to the rangers?" He needed to make sure he hadn't misunderstood something. He often misunderstood.

"Yep, that's the brilliant plan. I guess I should have given you a lying alert at the beginning," Agatha said. "Orville never lies," she told the others. "It's just not the way his brain works."

"The plan is to have Stu lie to the rangers?" Orville

repeated. "And to his parents and Ms. Winogrand?"

"Uh-huh," Agatha answered. "It'll fix everything. No one will end up getting in trouble. I'm brilliant, right? I mean, not as brilliant as you—"

"No," Orville said.

"Few people are. You're a complete genius," Agatha agreed.

"No. Stu can't lie to the rangers. It's wrong," Orville said. With the words, the pH level in his stomach rose, but he didn't think it had reached the healthy stomach pH of between one and two.

"What?" every person in the room other than Orville cried.

"It's wrong," Orville repeated.

"Orville, you know sometimes we have to lie a little when we're working a case," Agatha protested.

"You are not going to screw this up for me, retardo," Stu burst out.

"I could go to jail!" Jung exclaimed.

"My parents . . ." Clark let his words trail off.

"Orville, look at me," Agatha said. "And the rest of you please be quiet."

He turned his head toward her and forced himself to meet her gaze, even though it felt uncomfortable.

"Orville, there are bad lies, and there are good lies," Agatha said. "And there are times when it's okay to lie, remember? This lie will help Clark, and Jung, and Stu.

And it won't hurt anybody. Can you tell me one person it will hurt?"

"No. This is not a time when it's okay to lie." Orville was surprised at himself. He'd thought it would be hard to tell the difference between the okay-to-lie times and the not-okay times. But this wasn't hard at all. He was completely certain about it. "It's never okay to lie to the police. And the rangers are just like the police. If people lie to the police, it is likely that our whole society will eventually fail," Orville explained. "It's an entirely different situation from one in which you lie to give someone a compliment."

"Okay." Agatha's eyebrows were drawn together. "But you won't be doing the lying."

"That's right!" Stu cried. "I will. And I don't care about the society thing!"

"You don't even have to go to the ranger station. You don't have to do anything else," Agatha said. "How does that sound?"

The acid level increased in Orville's stomach again. He could feel the pH lowering. "It's wrong, Agatha. If Stu lies, I'll tell the rangers the truth myself," Orville answered.

"No way!" Stu blasted. "This is none of your business, moron. No one invited you to—"

"Shut up, Stu," Clark ordered.

Stu shut up.

"Orville's right." Clark stood up and faced Jung, Stu,

Agatha, and Orville. "We can't lie to the cops. And I'm not going to let Orville be the one to do the right thing while I try to hide from the consequences of my actions."

"What?" Stu whispered.

"I started this," Clark said. "And I'm going to tell the rangers the truth."

"Clark, you know what could happen to us," Jung protested.

"I know," Clark answered. "But maybe they'll go easier on us if we come forward. And even if they don't, I gotta do the right thing." He looked at Orville. "I keep thinking about you going into that cabin after Agatha—when you knew there was a wolf in there. You were seriously brave that day. You inspire me, man."

Orville felt warmth spread through his body. He thought he might be feeling proud. Clark had just paid *him* a compliment. "Thank you," he said.

"What are you talking about?" Stu demanded. "You're crazy!"

"I'm crazy to let you get to me," Clark retorted. "I can't believe I got myself into such a mess just because of a little twerp like you! Now I'm finally going to act my age and be the responsible one. I'm going to tell the rangers the truth, no matter how much trouble I get in. I'm not afraid."

Jung stood up, her eyes shining. "Then I'm going to the ranger station with you. We were in this together. We talk to them together." She grabbed Clark's hand.

Stu groaned and rolled his eyes, but nobody paid any attention to him.

"Oh, Jung. Do you know my cousin Billy Brown?" Agatha asked.

"Yeah. I think so. Kinda," Jung said. "Why?"

"Well, it seems like he had a great conversation with you by the drinking fountain," Agatha said. "And now he's in love. Do you think you could find a way to . . . um . . ."

"Turn the love into friendship?" Jung asked.

Agatha nodded.

"Sure," Jung said.

She and Clark started for the door, Agatha and Orville right behind them.

Stu didn't move.

"Get your butt out of that chair, Stu," Clark demanded.

Stu still didn't move. "You can go and be noble and everything. That doesn't mean I have to."

"We're just going to tell them what you did anyway, whether you're there or not," Jung said.

"And Orville and I will back them up," Agatha added.

"Fine. Losers," Stu said with a sneer. "Do what you want. I'm staying here and eating my brownies."

"I'll handle it," Clark said. He walked over, grabbed Stu's arm, yanked him out of his seat, and pulled him out the door.

Chapter 12

The city bus hit a bump, sending Agatha bouncing into the air. Orville bounced beside her. "They should fill those potholes up with Trixie Taffy if the town can't afford anything else," she said.

"The average temperature in Bottomless Lake from May to September would liquefy the taffy," Orville answered. "Then it is very likely the wheels of vehicles passing over it would pull it free."

"Huh. Good point." Agatha fell silent. That was unusual, she knew. But Orville didn't comment on it. The thing was, she had something to say to Orville, but she didn't quite know how to say it. And that was unusual too. She usually knew how to say pretty much anything. To anybody. Saying stuff was her raison d'être.

She shifted the bag of snacks she was holding from one hand to the other. She cleared her throat. She took a sip from the bottle of guaranteed Bottomless Lake water that Nana Wong sold in her store. Nana just didn't actually specify that the water came from the town of Bottomless Lake, not the lake of Bottomless Lake.

"Um, Orville, I just wanted to say that you were

right. You know, about Clark, Jung, and Stu needing to tell the rangers the truth," Agatha finally said.

"I know," Orville replied.

"And I was totally wrong to have told Stu to lie," she continued.

"I know," Orville said.

Agatha hoped that Orville's social skills class would cover accepting an apology at some point. She wasn't sure he'd know how to do it. But he completely deserved the apology from her whether he could handle it or not.

"I'm sorry about that," she said. "I got so wrapped up in solving the case that I wanted to make sure I solved *everything*—Clark's problem, Stu's problem, whatever. But our only job was to find Stu, and we did that. I shouldn't have tried to interfere with their situation. And I certainly shouldn't have told anyone to lie to the police."

"I know," Orville said.

"Anyway, I'm sorry. And I'm glad you were there to keep me from doing such a stupid thing."

"You are always there to keep me from doing stupid things," Orville said.

Agatha grinned. This was such a warm and fuzzy moment! "It was brave of you to stand up for the truth when you knew no one agreed with you," Agatha told him.

"I wasn't exhibiting any signs of fear," Orville told her.

"Doing something you're afraid of isn't the only kind of bravery," she replied. "You knew you were totally ruining the plan that would let Jung, Clark, and Stu get away with the kidnapping, right?"

"Yes," Orville answered.

Agatha pulled the cord that indicated they wanted the next stop. "Did you think about the possibility that they might get furious with you?" Actually, Agatha didn't usually care much if people got mad at her. People got mad at her a lot because she didn't think before she opened her mouth, her nana said. But that was about stuff like if she thought someone's haircut made them look like they had a sea anemone setting up house on their head or if she thought they were as stupid as a cracked plank. Not about colossal stuff.

"I just knew lying to the rangers was wrong," Orville answered.

"You're one rare and special individual, Benjamin Orville Wright. And I am proud to call you my friend."

The bus shuddered to a stop. The back door opened—after Agatha gave it a tiny kick—and she and Orville climbed out. "Do you see them?" she asked.

Orville put on a pair of sunglasses. "No."

"What's with the Terminator shades?" Agatha asked.

"UV rays are getting stronger each year. We are

going to be out in the sun for an extended period, and eye protection is very important." Orville handed Agatha a pair of sunglasses with round white frames.

"Very sixties. Very glam. Thanks." Agatha stuck them on. "Maybe they're a little farther down the road. Clark said they'd be traveling west." She turned toward Orville. "Which way is west?"

Orville pointed. They started walking alongside the road.

"Oh. Right. Where the sun is starting to go down. 'Cause the sun, it sets in the west," Agatha said.

The road curved, and when they rounded it, Agatha gave a squeal of delight. "It's Stu! It's Stu Frysley cleaning up trash. Hold this." She thrust the bag of snacks into Orville's hands, pulled off her backpack, rooted around inside, and found her camera.

"Smile, Stu!" Agatha pushed her sunglasses on top of her head and clicked away. Stu flung his arm in front of his face in the classic celebrity-who-has-done-something-really-really-really-stupid pose. "Aw, come on, Stu, don't be shy. Give it up for me," Agatha yelled.

Stu turned his back to her and bent down to add another piece of garbage to his sack. "Butt shot. Yeah, baby," Agatha cried.

Clark and Jung laughed from the other side of the street. "Let's go say hi to the non-mutants," Agatha suggested. She and Orville crossed over to them. "We brought you snacks. Take your pick. But if I were you, I wouldn't take the Trixie cookies. My nana only stocks them in the store because my uncle Jim makes them and he's family and Nana is all about the family. She wouldn't let me leave unless I took some away with me. Oh, and two of those pink popcorns are for me and Orville." Agatha pulled them out of the bag.

Jung took the last popcorn and Clark took a package of Trixie Sticks, which were like Pixie Sticks except— okay, they were exactly like Pixie Sticks except they had the Sea Monsteress on the side.

"How's the community service going?" Agatha asked.

"It's not jail," Jung said.

"And it's not juvie," Clark added. "Which means we're lovin' it. It was so cool of the rangers to set it up with our parents and the school and the Serve Your Community people. I'd happily haul trash from now until I leave for college. Forget about six months."

"Don't I get a snack?" Stu surfaced like a bad smell.

"If you let me take one picture without covering your face, you can have the cookies," Agatha said.

"Fine," Stu muttered. "Take it. I'm starving."

"Oh, and I need you to be holding a piece of trash. And I want your bag up nice and high," Agatha instructed.

Stu obeyed. "Perfect," Agatha told him. "Now, smile."

"Here, Stu. This will help. Look at Mr. Bunny." Clark pulled out the green eraser and waved it.

Stu grimaced. Agatha snapped.

"Back to work, you three," a man in a yellow Serve Your Community T-shirt called.

"Thanks for the treats, guys," Jung said. Clark gave Agatha and Orville a half salute. Stu stomped across the street without another word.

"Stool time," Agatha announced. She pulled three pieces of wood and a piece of canvas out of her backpack and made a seat for herself.

Orville took the same items out of his backpack, constructed a stool, and then sat down next to Agatha. She handed him a bag of pink popcorn and began eating from one herself. "This is what I call a show," she said, watching Stu pick up piece after piece of trash.

Agatha pulled a fresh bottle of water out of her backpack. "A toast," she said. She held up the bottle and waited until Orville held up his. "To the Wright and Wong detective team. We have now solved three out of three cases. We rock." She tapped Orville's bottle with hers, then took a long swig. "I knew Stu Frysley was our perp from the very first moment."

"Stu wasn't the perpetrator of the Stu-snatching," Orville said. "Clark and Jung planned the snatching, and Jung carried it out."

"Okay, yes, but Stu was the truly guilty one of the three. So I was right from the beginning," Agatha explained.

"He wasn't guilty of playing a prank or taking himself out of the tent," Orville told her.

How could Orville be so logical and not understand . . . logic? "Stu was really the bad guy in the situation. He was blackmailing Jung and Stu, remember? I could smell badness on Stu from day one. So I was right. And when I say I, I mean we, the team of Wright and Wong was right."

"But we weren't looking for a blackmailer," Orville replied.

Agatha felt her eyes begin to cross.

"Your hair looks pretty," Orville added.

Agatha ran her fingers through her thick dark hair. "Really? I used a different conditioner this morning. It's supposed to—" She stopped and stared at Orville. "Wait. You're just practicing for social skills class again, aren't you?"

"Yes," Orville answered.

Agatha shook her head. "I can't believe you got me again."